The Book of Dragons

THE BOOK OF
DRAGONS

SELECTED AND
ILLUSTRATED BY

Michael Hague

HarperCollins*Publishers*

For the Reuther family—
David, Margie, Kate, and Jacob

"The Dragon and the Enchanted Filly" from *Italian Folktales: Selected and Retold by Italo Calvino,* translated by George Martin, reprinted by permission of Harcourt Brace & Company. Copyright © 1956 by Guilio Einaudi editore s.p.a., English translation © 1980 by Harcourt Brace & Company.

"The Adventures of Eustace" from *Voyage of the Dawn Treader,* by C. S. Lewis, reprinted by permission of HarperCollins Publishers, Limited.

"Perseus and Andromeda" from *The Golden Fleece,* by Padraic Colum, reprinted by permission of Macmillan Books for Young Readers, an imprint of Simon & Schuster Children's Publishing Division. Copyright © 1921 by Macmillan Publishing Company; copyright renewed 1949 by Padraic Colum.

"Li Chi Slays the Serpent," by Kan Pao, from *Chinese Fairy Tales and Fantasies,* by Moss Roberts, reprinted by permission of Pantheon Books, Inc., a division of Random House, Inc. Copyright © 1979 by Moss Roberts.

"Bilbo Baggins and Smaug" from *The Hobbit,* by J. R. R. Tolkien, reprinted by permission of HarperCollins Publishers, Limited, and Houghton Mifflin Co. All rights reserved. Copyright © 1966 by J. R. R. Tolkien.

"The Devil and His Grandmother" from *The Complete Grimms' Fairy Tales,* by Jakob L. K. Grimm and Wilhelm K. Grimm, translated by Hunt & Stern. Copyright © 1944 by Pantheon Books, Inc.; copyright renewed 1972 by Random House, Inc.

"The Story of Wang Li," by Elizabeth Coatsworth, reprinted by permission of Kate Barnes and Margaret Beston.

"St. George and the Dragon," retold by William H. G. Kingston, reprinted by permission of The Limited Editions Club. Copyright © 1949 by The Limited Editions Club.

Watercolors were used for the full-color art. Pen and ink were used for the black-and-white art.
The text type is 14-point Centaur Monotype.

Copyright © 1995 by Michael Hague

Library of Congress Cataloging-in-Publication Data
The book of dragons / selected and illustrated by Michael Hague.
p. cm.
Summary: A collection of short stories featuring dragons, by such authors as Italo Calvino,
Kenneth Grahame, and Elizabeth Coatsworth.
ISBN 0-688-10879-2 — ISBN 0-06-075968-2 (pbk.)
1. Dragons—Juvenile fiction. 2. Children's stories. [1. Dragons—Fiction. 2. Fantasy.
3. Short stories.] I. Hague, Michael. PZ5.B638 1995 [Fic]—dc20 94-42958 CIP AC

CONTENTS

The Dragon and the Enchanted Filly

retold by Italo Calvino

THERE WAS ONCE a king and queen who had no children. The royal couple constantly prayed for a baby and gave generously to the poor. At last the queen found herself with child, and the king sent for astrologers to find out if it would be a boy or a girl and under what star it would be born. The astrologers replied, "You will have a boy, who the minute he turns twenty will take a wife, and in the same instant he will slay her. Otherwise he would turn into a dragon." The king and queen were all smiles when the astrologers informed them they would have a son who would marry at the outset of his twentieth year. But upon hearing the rest of the prophecy they burst into tears.

The son was born and grew into a fine young man. That was no little

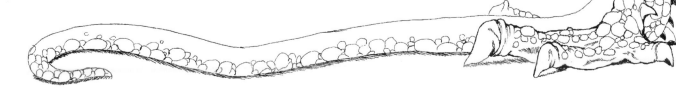

comfort to his parents, who nevertheless shuddered at the thought of his terrible fate. As his twentieth birthday approached, they sought a wife for him and asked for the hand of the queen of England.

Now the queen of England had a talking filly who told her owner everything and was, beyond all doubt, her best friend. As soon as the queen became engaged, she spread the word to the filly. "You have no cause to rejoice," replied the filly, a bewitched animal who knew everything. "The truth of the matter is…" and she revealed the prince's strange destiny. The queen was horrified and wondered what she should now do. "Listen carefully," said the filly. "Tell your bridegroom's father the queen of England will not ride to the wedding in a carriage but on horseback. Come wedding day, you will mount me and proceed to the church. The instant I paw the ground, throw your arms around my neck and leave everything to me."

In the wedding procession the filly, draped in gala trappings, stood beside the bridegroom's carriage, while on her sat the queen of England in her wedding dress. Every now and then the queen peered through the carriage window at the bridegroom with a sword on his lap and at her in-laws holding watches and awaiting the exact time when he had been born. Suddenly the filly pawed the ground with all her might, then sped off like lightning, with the bride holding on for dear life. The fatal hour had struck, and the bridegroom's parents dropped their watches. Right before their eyes the king's son had turned into a dragon, sending king, queen, and courtiers fleeing for their lives from the overturned carriage.

The filly reached a farmhouse and drew to a halt. "Dismount," she told the queen, "and go in and tell the farmer to give you his clothes in exchange for your royal ones." The farmer could hardly believe he was getting a real queen's dress, and a wedding dress at that. In exchange, he gave her his coarse shirt and breeches. The queen came back out dressed as a farmer, jumped into the saddle, and continued on her way.

They came to the palace of a second king, and the filly said, "Go to the stables and see if they'll engage you as a stableboy." She did, impressing the people as a bright boy who also had that fine filly, so they said, "We'll hire you with your filly to work here with us."

Now the king had a son the girl's age exactly. The boy no sooner saw the new groom than a certain thought struck him, which he confided to his mother. "Mamma, I may be wrong, but I believe that new stableboy is a girl and one that appeals to me."

"No, no," replied the mother, "you're all wrong. If you want to find out for sure, take him to the garden and show him the flowers. If he makes a bouquet, then you'll know your stableboy is actually a girl. If he pulls a flower and sticks it in his mouth, he's a man."

The prince called the stableboy into the garden and said, "Would you like to make a bouquet of flowers?"

But the filly who knew everything had already warned the false stableboy, who replied, "No, thanks, I don't care much for flowers," and pulled a blossom and stuck it in her mouth.

"What did I tell you? He's a man for sure," replied the queen when the prince related the incident.

"I don't care what you say, Mamma. I'm more convinced than ever that the stableboy is really a girl."

"Try something else, then: invite him to the table to cut the bread. If he holds it up to his chest, your stableboy is actually a girl. If he holds it away from him to cut it, then he's a man."

This time too the filly warned her mistress, who held the bread away from her like a man. The prince was still not convinced, though.

"The only thing left," said his mother, "is to see him fence. Arrange a match with him."

The filly taught the girl all the subtleties of fencing, but concluded, "This time, my dear, you will be found out."

No fault could ever be found with her fencing, but in the end she fainted from exhaustion. And that way they finally discovered she was a girl. The prince was so deeply in love by now that he resolved at all costs to marry her.

"Marry her without any idea who she is?" exclaimed his mother.

They asked her to tell her story, and upon learning that she was the queen of England, the prince's mother made no objections to the wedding, which was celebrated with great pomp.

A little later, the new wife found herself with child, when the king was summoned to war. But being an old man, he sent his son in his place. The prince urged his parents to write him as soon as the baby was born, mounted his wife's filly, and rode off to battle. Before leaving, however, the filly gave her mistress three hairs from her mane, saying, "Hide these in your bosom. Break them in an emergency, and I'll come to your aid."

In due time the princess gave birth to twins, a boy and a girl, who were the most beautiful children you ever saw. The king and queen wrote their son the good news at once. Now as the messenger was riding to the prince with the letter, a dragon lay in wait for him midway to the battlefield. It was none other than the other king's son who had turned into a monster on his wedding day. Seeing the messenger approach, it blew its noxious breath down the road, and the man fell from his saddle in a deep sleep. Then the dragon pulled the letter from the messenger's pocket, read it, and forged a new one saying the princess had borne two dogs, a male and a female, thus turning the whole town against her. This letter went into the pocket of the messenger, who, finding nothing amiss upon awaking, got back onto his horse and rode to the prince.

When the prince read the letter, he turned as white as a sheet, but said

nothing. He sat down immediately and wrote a reply: "Be they male dogs or females, keep them for me and take good care of my wife."

On the way back, the messenger was again spotted by the dragon and put to sleep by its breath as he came down the road. The dragon replaced the letter the messenger bore with one that read: "Burn wife and children at the stake in the town square. If king and queen do not comply, they too shall go up in flames."

Such a reply threw the town into alarm. What was the meaning of the prince's fury? But instead of burning those innocent souls, the king and queen put the princess into a boat along with the children, two nurses, food, water, and four oarsmen, and secretly launched them on the sea. Then they carried to the town square three dummies resembling the princess and her babies and set them afire. The citizens, who had grown to love the princess, were outraged and vowed revenge.

The princess sailed across the sea and was put ashore with her babies. She was walking along the deserted strand, when before her loomed the dragon. She had already given herself and the children up for doomed, when she remembered the three hairs from her filly's mane. She pulled them from her bosom, broke one, and saw an impenetrable thicket instantly spring up around her. But the dragon plunged into it and twisted his way right on through. She broke another hair, and out gushed a river wide and deep. The dragon had a time in the swift current, but he finally got across the river as well. She frantically broke the last hair as the dragon was about to seize her, and a tongue of fire shot up and expanded into a mighty fire. But the dragon passed through the fire, too, and had her in his hands, when onto the shore galloped the filly.

They faced one another, filly and dragon, and then began to fight. The dragon was taller, but the filly reared and kicked and bit so furiously that she laid him low and crushed him to bits. The princess rushed up to embrace the filly, but her joy was shortlived, for the filly closed her eyes, hung her head, and dropped lifeless to the ground. The princess wept as though she had lost her own sister, recalling all that the filly had done for her.

She was there weeping with her children, when she happened to look up and see a large palace she didn't remember seeing before. Moving closer, she noticed a beautiful lady at a window motioning to her to come inside. She entered with her children, and the lady embraced her, saying, "You don't recognize me, but I'm the filly. I was under a spell and couldn't change back into a woman until I'd slain a dragon. When you broke the hairs of my mane, I left your husband on the battlefield and ran to you. Killing the dragon, I broke the spell."

Let's leave them for the time being and turn to the husband when he saw the filly flee from the battlefield. He thought to himself, Something must have happened to my wife! and hurried to win the war so he could go home.

When he got back to town, all the citizens rose up against him. "Tyrant! Monster!" they screamed. "What crime had that poor woman and her children committed?" He couldn't for the life of him understand what the people were talking about. When his father and mother, wrathful and grief-stricken, produced the letter received from him, he said, "This is not from me!" He showed them the letter he had received, and they realized then that both letters had been forged by no telling whom.

After rounding up the mariners who had rowed his wife to that deserted shore, the prince put out to sea with them immediately. He came to the spot where they had disembarked, saw the dead dragon and then the dead filly, and lost all hope. But while he was weeping, he heard his name called: it was the beautiful lady at the palace window. He went inside, and the lady announced she was the filly and led him into a room, where he found his

wife and children. They hugged and kissed, wept and cried. Then, together with the beautiful lady who'd been a filly, they departed. Everyone was overjoyed to have them back, and from that time on they were always together and as happy as happy could be.

The Adventures of Eustace

from *Voyage of the Dawn Treader*

by C. S. Lewis

MOST OF US know what we should expect to find in a dragon's lair, but, as I said before, Eustace had read only the wrong books. They had a lot to say about exports and imports and governments and drains, but they were weak on dragons. That is why he was so puzzled at the surface on which he was lying. Parts of it were too prickly to be stones and too hard to be thorns, and there seemed to be a great many round, flat things, and it all clinked when he moved. There was light enough at the cave's mouth to examine it by. And of course Eustace found it to be what any of us could have told him in advance—treasure. There were crowns (those were the prickly things), coins, rings, bracelets, ingots, cups, plates, and gems.

Eustace (unlike most boys) has never thought much of treasure but he saw at once the use it would be in this new world which he had so foolishly stumbled into through the picture in Lucy's bedroom at home. "They don't have any tax here," he said. "And you don't have to give treasure to the government. With some of this stuff I could have quite a decent time here—perhaps in Calormen. It sounds the least phony of these countries. I wonder how much I can carry? That bracelet now—those things in it are probably diamonds—I'll slip that on my own wrist. Too big, but not if I push it right up here above my elbow. Then fill my pockets with diamonds—that's easier than gold. I wonder when this infernal rain's going to let up?" He got into a less uncomfortable part of the pile, where it was mostly coins, and settled down to wait. But a bad fright, when once it is over, and especially a bad fright following a mountain walk, leaves you very tired. Eustace fell asleep.

What woke him was a pain in his arm. The moon was shining in at the mouth of the cave, and the bed of treasures seemed to have grown much more comfortable: in fact he could hardly feel it at all. He was puzzled by the pain in his arm at first, but presently it occurred to him that the bracelet which he had shoved up above his elbow had become strangely tight. His arm must have swollen while he was asleep (it was his left arm).

He moved his right arm in order to feel his left, but stopped before he had moved it an inch and bit his lip in terror. For just in front of him, and a little on his right, where the moonlight fell clear on the floor of the cave, he saw a hideous shape moving. He knew that shape: it was a dragon's claw. It had moved as he moved his hand and became still when he stopped moving his hand.

"Oh, what a fool I've been," thought Eustace. "Of course, the brute had a mate and it's lying beside me."

For several minutes he did not dare to move a muscle. He saw two thin columns of smoke going up before his eyes, black against the moonlight; just as there had been smoke coming from the other dragon's nose before it died. This was so alarming that he held his breath. The two columns of smoke vanished. When he could hold his breath no longer he let it out stealthily; instantly two jets of smoke appeared again. But even yet he had no idea of the truth.

Presently he decided that he would edge very cautiously to his left and try to creep out of the cave. Perhaps the creature was asleep—and anyway it was his only chance. But of course before he edged to the left he looked to the left. Oh horror! There was a dragon's claw on that side, too.

No one will blame Eustace if at this moment he shed tears. He was surprised at the size of his own tears as he saw them splashing on to the treasure in front of him. They also seemed strangely hot; steam went up from them.

But there was no good crying. He must try to crawl out from between the two dragons. He began extending his right arm. The dragon's foreleg and claw on his right went through exactly the same motion. Then he thought he would try his left. The dragon limb on that side moved, too.

Two dragons, one on each side, mimicking whatever he did! His nerve broke and he simply made a bolt for it.

There was such a clatter and rasping, and clinking of gold, and grinding of stones, as he rushed out of the cave that he thought they were both following him. He daren't look back. He rushed to the pool. The twisted shape of the dead dragon lying in the moonlight would have been enough to frighten anyone but now he hardly noticed it. His idea was to get into the water.

But just as he reached the edge of the pool two things happened. First of all it came over him like a thunderclap that he had been running on all fours—and why on earth had he been doing that? And secondly, as he bent

towards the water, he thought for a second that yet another dragon was staring up at him out of the pool. But in an instant he realized the truth. That dragon face in the pool was his own reflection. There was no doubt of it. It moved as he moved: it opened and shut its mouth as he opened and shut his.

He had turned into a dragon while he was asleep. Sleeping on a dragon's hoard with greedy, dragonish thoughts in his heart, he had become a dragon himself.

That explained everything. There had been no two dragons beside him in the cave. The claws to right and left had been his own right and left claws. The two columns of smoke had been coming from his own nostrils. As for the pain in his left arm (or what had been his left arm) he could now see what had happened by squinting with his left eye. The bracelet which had fitted very nicely on the upper arm of a boy was far too small for the thick, stumpy foreleg of a dragon. It had sunk deeply into his scaly flesh and there was a throbbing bulge on each side of it. He tore at the place with his dragon's teeth but could not get it off.

In spite of the pain, his first feeling was one of relief. There was nothing to be afraid of any more. He was a terror himself now and nothing in the world but a knight (and not all of these) would dare to attack him. He could get even with Caspian and Edmund now. . . .

But the moment he thought this he realized that he didn't want to. He wanted to be friends. He wanted to get back among humans and talk and laugh and share things. He realized that he was a monster cut off from the whole human race. An appalling loneliness came over him. He began to see the others had not really been friends at all. He began to wonder if he himself had been such a nice person as he had always supposed. He longed for their voices. He would have been grateful for a kind word even from Reepicheep.

When he thought of this the poor dragon that had been Eustace lifted up its voice and wept. A powerful dragon crying its eyes out under the moon in a deserted valley is a sight and a sound hardly to be imagined.

Perseus and Andromeda

by Padraic Colum

IN ETHIOPIA, WHICH is at the other side of Libya, there ruled a king whose name was Cepheus. This king had permitted his queen to boast that she was more beautiful than the nymphs of the sea. In punishment for the queen's impiety and for the king's folly Poseidon sent a monster out of the sea to waste that country. Every year the monster came, destroying more and more of the country of Ethiopia. Then the king asked of an oracle what he should do to save his land and his people. The oracle spoke of a dreadful thing that he would have to do—he would have to sacrifice his daughter, the beautiful Princess Andromeda.

The king was forced by his savage people to take the maiden Andromeda and chain her to a rock on the seashore, leaving her there

for the monster to devour her, satisfying himself with that prey.

Perseus, flying near, heard the maiden's laments. He saw her lovely body bound with chains to the rock. He came near her, taking the cap of darkness off his head. She saw him, and she bent her head in shame, for she thought that he would think that it was for some dreadful fault of her own that she had been left chained in that place.

Her father had stayed near. Perseus saw him, and called to him, and bade him tell why the maiden was chained to the rock. The king told Perseus of the sacrifice that he had been forced to make. Then Perseus came near the maiden, and he saw how she looked at him with pleading eyes.

Then Perseus made her father promise that he would give Andromeda to him for his wife if he should slay the sea monster. Gladly Cepheus promised this. Then Perseus once again drew his sickle-sword; by the rock to which Andromeda was still chained he waited for sight of the sea monster.

It came rolling in from the open sea, a shapeless and unsightly thing. With the shoes of flight upon his feet Perseus rose above it. The monster saw his shadow upon the water, and savagely it went to attack the shadow. Perseus swooped down as an eagle swoops down; with his sickle-sword he attacked it, and he struck the hook through the monster's shoulder. Terribly it reared up from the sea. Perseus rose over it, escaping its wide-opened mouth with its treble rows of fangs. Again he swooped and struck at it. Its hide was covered all over with hard scales and with the shells of sea things, but Perseus's sword struck through it. It reared up again, spouting water mixed with blood. On a rock near the rock that Andromeda was chained to Perseus alighted. The monster, seeing him, bellowed and rushed swiftly through the water to overwhelm him. As it reared up he plunged the sword again and again into its body. Down into the water the monster sank, and water mixed with blood was spouted up from the depths into which it sank.

Then was Andromeda loosed from her chains. Perseus, the conqueror, lifted up the fainting maiden and carried her back to the king's palace. And Cepheus there renewed his promise to give her in marriage to her deliverer.

Perseus went on his way. He came to the hidden valley where the nymphs had their dwelling place, and he restored to them the three magic treasures that they had given him—the cap of darkness, the shoes of flight, and the magic pouch. And these treasures are still there, and the hero who can win his way to the nymphs may have them as Perseus had them.

Again he returned to the place where he had found Andromeda chained. With face averted he drew forth the Gorgon's head from where he had hidden it between the rocks. He made a bag for it out of the horny skin of the monster he had slain. Then, carrying his tremendous trophy, he went to the palace of King Cepheus to claim his bride.

from

The Reluctant Dragon

by Kenneth Grahame

THE HIGHER PORTIONS of the ground were now black with sightseers, and presently a sound of cheering and a waving of handkerchiefs told that something was visible to them which the Boy, far up towards the dragon-end of the line as he was, could not yet see. A minute more and St. George's red plumes topped the hill, as the Saint rode slowly forth on the great level space which stretched up to the grim mouth of the cave. Very gallant and beautiful he looked, on his tall war-horse, his golden armor glancing in the sun, his great spear held erect, the little white pennon, crimson-crossed, fluttering at its point. He drew rein and remained motionless. The lines of spectators began to give back a little, nervously;

and even the boys in front stopped pulling hair and cuffing each other, and leaned forward expectant.

"Now then, dragon!" muttered the Boy impatiently, fidgeting where he sat. He need not have distressed himself, had he only known. The dramatic possibilities of the thing had tickled the dragon immensely, and he had been up from an early hour, preparing for his first public appearance with as much heartiness as if the years had run backwards, and he had been again a little dragonlet, playing with his sisters on the floor of their mother's cave, at the game of saints-and-dragons, in which the dragon was bound to win.

A low muttering, mingled with snorts, now made itself heard; rising to a bellowing roar that seemed to fill the plain. Then a cloud of smoke obscured the mouth of the cave, and out of the midst of it the dragon himself, shining, sea-blue, magnificent, pranced splendidly forth; and everybody said, "Oo-oo-oo!" as if he had been a mighty rocket! His scales were glittering, his long spiky tail lashed his sides, his claws tore up the turf and sent it flying high over his back, and smoke and fire incessantly jetted from his angry nostrils. "Oh, well done, dragon!" cried the Boy, excitedly. "Didn't think he had it in him!" he added to himself.

St. George lowered his spear, bent his head, dug his heels into his horse's sides, and came thundering over the turf. The dragon charged with a roar and a squeal—a great blue whirling combination of coils and snorts and clashing jaws and spikes and fire.

"Missed!" yelled the crowd. There was a moment's entanglement of golden armor and blue-green coils, and spiky tail, and then the great horse, tearing at his bit, carried the Saint, his spear swung high in the air, almost up to the mouth of the cave.

The dragon sat down and barked viciously, while St. George with difficulty pulled his horse round into position.

"End of Round One!" thought the Boy. "How well they managed it! But I hope the Saint won't get excited. I can trust the dragon all right. What a regular play-actor the fellow is!"

St. George had at last prevailed on his horse to stand steady, and was looking round him as he wiped his brow. Catching sight of the Boy, he smiled and nodded, and held up three fingers for an instant.

"It seems to be all planned out," said the Boy to himself. "Round Three is to be the finishing one, evidently. Wish it could have lasted a bit longer. Whatever's that old fool of a dragon up to now?"

The dragon was employing the interval in giving a ramping performance for the benefit of the crowd. Ramping, it should be explained, consists in running round and round in a wide circle and sending waves and ripples of movement along the whole length of your spine, from your pointed ears right down to the spike at the end of your long tail. When you are covered

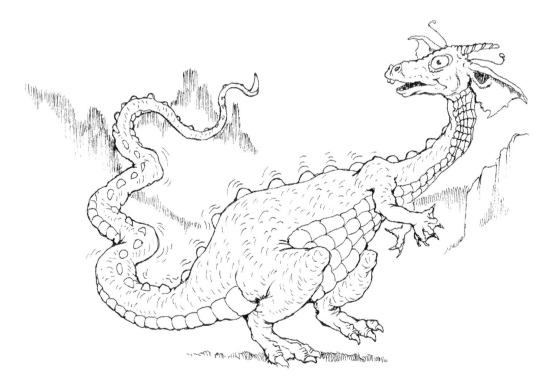

with blue scales, the effect is particularly pleasing; and the Boy recollected the dragon's recently expressed wish to become a social success.

St. George now gathered up his reins and began to move forward, dropping the point of his spear and settling himself firmly in the saddle.

"Time!" yelled everybody excitedly; and the dragon, leaving off his ramping, sat up on end, and began to leap from one side to the other with huge ungainly bounds, whooping like a Red Indian. This naturally disconcerted the horse, who swerved violently, the Saint only just saving himself by the mane; and as they shot past, the dragon delivered a vicious snap at the horse's tail which sent the poor beast careering madly far over the Downs, so that the language of the Saint, who had lost a stirrup, was fortunately inaudible to the general assemblage.

Round Two evoked audible evidence of friendly feeling towards the dragon. The spectators were not slow to appreciate a combatant who could hold his own so well and clearly wanted to show good sport; and many encouraging remarks reached the ears of our friend as he strutted to and fro, his chest thrust out and his tail in the air, hugely enjoying his new popularity.

St. George had dismounted and was tightening his girths, and telling his horse, with quite an Oriental flow of imagery, exactly what he thought of him, and his relations, and his conduct on the present occasion; so the Boy made his way down to the Saint's end of the line, and held his spear for him.

"It's been a jolly fight, St. George!" he said with a sigh. "Can't you let it last a bit longer?"

"Well, I think I'd better not," replied the Saint. "The fact is, your simpleminded old friend's getting conceited, now they've begun cheering him, and he'll forget all about the arrangement and take to playing the fool, and there's no telling where he would stop. I'll just finish him off this round."

He swung himself into the saddle and took his spear from the Boy. "Now don't be afraid," he added kindly. "I've marked my spot exactly, and *he's* sure to give me all the assistance in his power, because he knows it's his only chance of being asked to the banquet!"

St. George now shortened his spear, bringing the butt well up under his arm; and, instead of galloping as before, trotted smartly towards the dragon, who crouched at his approach, flicking his tail till it cracked in the air like a great cart whip. The Saint wheeled as he neared his opponent and circled warily round him, keeping his eye on the spare place; while the dragon, adopting similar tactics, paced with caution round the same circle, occasionally feinting with his head. So the two sparred for an opening, while the spectators maintained a breathless silence.

Though the round lasted for some minutes, the end was so swift that all the Boy saw was a lightning movement of the Saint's arm, and then a whirl and a confusion of spines, claws, tail, and flying bits of turf. The dust cleared away, the spectators whooped and ran in cheering, and the Boy made out that the dragon was down, pinned to the earth by the spear, while St. George had dismounted, and stood astride of him.

It all seemed so genuine that the Boy ran in breathlessly, hoping the dear old dragon wasn't really hurt. As he approached, the dragon lifted one large eyelid, winked solemnly, and collapsed again. He was held fast to earth by the neck, but the Saint had hit him in the spare place agreed upon, and it didn't even seem to tickle.

"Bain't you goin' to cut 'is 'ed orf, master?" asked one of the applauding crowd. He had backed the dragon, and naturally felt a trifle sore.

"Well, not *today*, I think," replied St. George, pleasantly. "You see, that can be done at *any* time. There's no hurry at all. I think we'll all go down to the village first, and have some refreshment, and then I'll give him a good talking-to, and you'll find he'll be a very different dragon!"

The Flower Queen's Daughter

retold by Andrew Lang

A YOUNG PRINCE was riding one day through a meadow that stretched for miles in front of him, when he came to a deep open ditch. He was turning aside to avoid it, when he heard the sound of someone crying in the ditch. He dismounted from his horse, and stepped along in the direction the sound came from. To his astonishment he found an old woman, who begged him to help her out of the ditch. The Prince bent down and lifted her out of her living grave, asking her at the same time how she had managed to get there.

"My son," answered the old woman, "I am a very poor woman, and soon after midnight I set out for the neighboring town in order to sell my eggs in the market on the following morning; but I lost my way in the dark, and fell into this deep ditch, where I might have remained for ever but for your kindness."

Then the Prince said to her, "You can hardly walk; I will put you on my horse and lead you home. Where do you live?"

"Over there, at the edge of the forest in the little hut you see in the distance," replied the old woman.

The Prince lifted her on to his horse, and soon they reached the hut, where the old woman got down, and turning to the Prince said, "Just wait a moment, and I will give you something." And she disappeared into her hut, but returned very soon and said, "You are a mighty Prince, but at the same time you have a kind heart, which deserves to be rewarded. Would you like to have the most beautiful woman in the world for your wife?"

"Most certainly I would," replied the Prince.

So the old woman continued, "The most beautiful woman in the whole world is the daughter of the Queen of the Flowers, who has been captured by a dragon. If you wish to marry her, you must first set her free, and this I will help you to do. I will give you this little bell: if you ring it once, the King of the Eagles will appear; if you ring it twice, the King of the Foxes will come to you; and if you ring it three times, you will see the King of the Fishes by your side. These will help you if you are in any difficulty. Now farewell, and heaven prosper your undertaking." She handed him the little bell, and there disappeared hut and all, as though the earth had swallowed her up.

Then it dawned on the Prince that he had been speaking to a good fairy, and putting the little bell carefully in his pocket, he rode home and told his father that he meant to set the daughter of the Flower Queen free, and intended setting out on the following day into the wide world in search of the maid.

So the next morning the Prince mounted his fine horse and left his home. He had roamed round the world for a whole year, and his horse had died of exhaustion, while he himself had suffered much from want and misery, but still he had come on no trace of her he was in search of. At last one day he came to a hut, in front of which sat a very old man. The Prince asked him, "Do you not know where the Dragon lives who keeps the daughter of the Flower Queen prisoner?"

"No, I do not," answered the old man. "But if you go straight along this road for a year, you will reach a hut where my father lives, and possibly he may be able to tell you."

The Prince thanked him for his information, and continued his journey for a whole year along the same road, and at the end of it came to the little hut, where he found a very old man. He asked him the same question, and the old man answered, "No, I do not know where the Dragon lives. But go straight along this road for another year, and you will come to a hut in which my father lives. I know he can tell you."

And so the Prince wandered on for another year, always on the same road, and at last reached the hut where he found the third old man. He put the same question to him as he had put to his son and grandson; but this time the old man answered, "The Dragon lives up there on the mountain, and he has just begun his year of sleep. For one whole year he is always awake, and the next he sleeps. But if you wish to see the Flower Queen's daughter go up the second mountain: the Dragon's old mother lives there, and she has a ball every night, to which the Flower Queen's daughter goes regularly."

So the Prince went up the second mountain, where he found a castle all made of gold with diamond windows. He opened the big gate leading into the courtyard, and was just going to walk in, when seven dragons rushed on him and asked him what he wanted.

The Prince replied, "I have heard so much of the beauty and kindness

of the Dragon's Mother, and would like to enter her service."

This flattering speech pleased the dragons, and the eldest of them said, "Well, you may come with me, and I will take you to the Mother Dragon."

They entered the castle and walked through twelve splendid halls, all made of gold and diamonds. In the twelfth room they found the Mother Dragon seated on a diamond throne. She was the ugliest woman under the sun, and, added to it all, she had three heads. Her appearance was a great shock to the Prince, and so was her voice, which was like the croaking of many ravens. She asked him, "Why have you come here?"

The Prince answered at once, "I have heard so much of your beauty and kindness, that I would very much like to enter your service."

"Very well," said the Mother Dragon; "but if you wish to enter my service, you must first lead my mare out to the meadow and look after her for three days; but if you don't bring her home safely every evening, we will eat you up."

The Prince undertook the task and led the mare out to the meadow. But no sooner had they reached the grass than she vanished. The Prince sought for her in vain, and at last in despair sat down on a big stone and contemplated his sad fate. As he sat thus lost in thought, he noticed an eagle flying over his head. Then he suddenly bethought him of his little bell, and taking it out of his pocket he rang it once. In a moment he heard a rustling sound in the air beside him, and the King of the Eagles sank at his feet.

"I know what you want of me," the bird said. "You are looking for the Mother Dragon's mare who is galloping about among the clouds. I will summon all the eagles of the air together, and order them to catch the mare and bring her to you." And with these words the King of the Eagles flew away. Towards evening the Prince heard a mighty rushing sound in the air, and when he looked up he saw thousands of eagles driving the mare before them. They sank at his feet on to the ground and gave the mare over to him.

Then the Prince rode home to the old Mother Dragon, who was full of wonder when she saw him, and said, "You have succeeded today in looking after my mare, and as a reward you shall come to my ball tonight." She gave him at the same time a cloak made of copper, and led him to a big room where several young he-dragons and she-dragons were dancing together. Here, too, was the Flower Queen's beautiful daughter. Her dress was woven out of the most lovely flowers in the world, and her complexion was like lilies and roses. As the Prince was dancing with her he managed to whisper in her ear, "I have come to set you free!"

Then the beautiful girl said to him, "If you succeed in bringing the mare back safely the third day, ask the Mother Dragon to give you a foal of the mare as a reward."

The ball came to an end at midnight, and early next morning the Prince again led the Mother Dragon's mare out into the meadow. But again she vanished before his eyes. Then he took out his little bell and rang it twice.

In a moment the King of the Foxes stood before him and said: "I know already what you want, and will summon all the foxes of the world together to find the mare who has hidden herself in a hill."

With these words the King of the Foxes disappeared, and in the evening many thousand foxes brought the mare to the Prince.

Then he rode home to the Mother Dragon, from whom he received this time a cloak made of silver, and again she led him to the ballroom.

The Flower Queen's daughter was delighted to see him safe and sound, and when they were dancing together she whispered in his ear: "If you succeed again tomorrow, wait for me with the foal in the meadow. After the ball we will fly away together."

On the third day the Prince led the mare to the meadow again; but once more she vanished before his eyes. The Prince took out his little bell and rang it three times.

In a moment the King of the Fishes appeared, and said to him: "I know quite well what you want me to do, and I will summon all the fishes of the sea together, and tell them to bring you back the mare, who is hiding herself in a river."

Towards evening the mare was returned to him, and when he led her home to the Mother Dragon she said to him:

"You are a brave youth, and I will make you my body-servant. But what shall I give you as a reward to begin with?"

The Prince begged for a foal of the mare, which the Mother Dragon at once gave him, and over and above, a cloak made of gold, for she had fallen in love with him because he had praised her beauty.

So in the evening he appeared at the ball in his golden cloak; but before the entertainment was over he slipped away, and went straight to the stables, where he mounted his foal and rode out into the meadow to wait for the Flower Queen's daughter. Towards midnight the beautiful girl appeared, and placing her in front of him on his horse, the Prince and she flew like the wind till they reached the Flower Queen's dwelling. But the dragons had noticed their flight, and woke their brother out of his year's sleep. He flew into a terrible rage when he heard what had happened, and determined to lay siege to the Flower Queen's palace; but the Queen caused a forest of flowers as high as the sky to grow up round her dwelling, through which no one could force a way.

When the Flower Queen heard that her daughter wanted to marry the Prince, she said to him: "I will give my consent to your marriage gladly, but my daughter can only stay with you in summer. In winter, when everything is dead and the ground covered with snow, she must come and live with me in my palace underground." The Prince consented to this, and led his beautiful bride home, where the wedding was held with great pomp and magnificence. The young couple lived happily together till winter came, when the

Flower Queen's daughter departed and went home to her mother. In summer she returned to her husband, and their life of joy and happiness began again, and lasted till the approach of winter, when the Flower Queen's daughter went back again to her mother. This coming and going continued all her life long, and in spite of it they always lived happily together.

Li Chi Slays
the Serpent

by Kan Pao

I N F U K I E N, IN the ancient state of Yüeh, stands the Yung mountain range, whose peaks sometimes reach a height of many miles. To the northwest there is a cleft in the mountains once inhabited by a giant serpent seventy or eighty feet long and wider than the span of ten hands. It kept the local people in a state of constant terror and had already killed many commandants from the capital city and many magistrates and officers of nearby towns. Offerings of oxen and sheep did not appease the monster. By entering men's dreams and making its wishes known through mediums, it demanded young girls of twelve or thirteen to feast on.

Helpless, the commandant and the magistrates selected daughters of bondmaids or criminals and kept them until the appointed dates. One day

in the eighth month of every year, they would deliver a girl to the mouth of the monster's cave, and the serpent would come out and swallow the victim. This continued for nine years until nine girls had been devoured.

In the tenth year the officials had again begun to look for a girl to hold in readiness for the appointed time. A man of Chiang Lo county, Li Tan, had raised six daughters and no sons. Chi, his youngest girl, responded to the search for a victim by volunteering. Her parents refused to allow it, but she said, "Dear parents, you have no one to depend on, for having brought forth six daughters and not a single son, it is as if you were childless. I could never compare with Ti Jung of the Han Dynasty, who offered herself as a bondmaid to the emperor in exchange for her father's life. I cannot take care of you in your old age; I only waste your good food and clothes. Since I'm no use to you alive, why shouldn't I give up my life a little sooner? What could be wrong in selling me to gain a bit of money for yourselves?" But the father and mother loved her too much to consent, so she went in secret.

The volunteer then asked the authorities for a sharp sword and a snake-hunting dog. When the appointed day of the eighth month arrived, she seated herself in the temple, clutching the sword and leading the dog. First she took several pecks of rice balls moistened with malt sugar and placed them at the mouth of the serpent's cave.

The serpent appeared. Its head was as large as a rice barrel; its eyes were like mirrors two feet across. Smelling the fragrance of the rice balls, it opened its mouth to eat them. Then Li Chi unleashed the snake-hunting dog, which bit hard into the serpent. Li Chi herself came up from behind and scored the serpent with several deep cuts. The wounds hurt so terribly that the monster leaped into the open and died.

Li Chi went into the serpent's cave and recovered the skulls of the nine victims. She sighed as she brought them out, saying, "For your timidity you were devoured. How pitiful!" Slowly she made her way homeward.

The king of Yüeh learned of these events and made Li Chi his queen. He appointed her father magistrate of Chiang Lo county, and her mother and elder sisters were given riches. From that time forth, the district was free of monsters. Ballads celebrating Li Chi survive to this day.

Bilbo Baggins
and Smaug

from *The Hobbit*

by J. R. R. Tolkien

THE SUN WAS shining when he started, but it was as dark as night in the tunnel. The light from the door, almost closed, soon faded as he went down. So silent was his going that smoke on a gentle wind could hardly have surpassed it, and he was inclined to feel a bit proud of himself as he drew near the lower door. There was only the very faintest glow to be seen.

"Old Smaug is weary and asleep," he thought. "He can't see me and he won't hear me. Cheer up Bilbo!" He had forgotten or had never heard about dragons' sense of smell. It is also an awkward fact that they can keep half an eye open watching while they sleep, if they are suspicious.

Smaug certainly looked fast asleep, almost dead and dark, with scarcely

a snore more than a whiff of unseen steam, when Bilbo peeped once more from the entrance. He was just about to step out on to the floor when he caught a sudden thin and piercing ray of red from under the dropping lid of Smaug's left eye. He was only pretending to sleep! He was watching the tunnel entrance! Hurriedly Bilbo stepped back and blessed the luck of his ring. Then Smaug spoke.

"Well, thief! I smell you and I feel your air. I hear your breath. Come along! Help yourself again, there is plenty and to spare!"

But Bilbo was not quite so unlearned in dragon-lore as all that, and if Smaug hoped to get him to come nearer so easily he was disappointed. "No thank you, O Smaug the Tremendous!" he replied. "I did not come for presents. I only wished to have a look at you and see if you were truly as great as tales say. I did not believe them."

"Do you now?" said the dragon somewhat flattered, even though he did not believe a word of it.

"Truly songs and tales fall utterly short of the reality, O Smaug the Chiefest and Greatest of Calamities," replied Bilbo.

"You have nice manners for a thief and a liar," said the dragon. "You seem familiar with my name, but I don't seem to remember smelling you before. Who are you and where do you come from, may I ask?"

"You may indeed! I come from under the hill, and under the hills and over the hills my paths led. And through the air. I am he that walks unseen."

"So I can well believe," said Smaug, "but that is hardly your usual name."

"I am the clue-finder, the web-cutter, the stinging fly. I was chosen for the lucky number."

"Lovely titles!" sneered the dragon. "But lucky numbers don't always come off."

"I am he that buries his friends alive and drowns them and draws them

alive again from the water. I came from the end of a bag, but no bag went over me."

"These don't sound so creditable," scoffed Smaug.

"I am the friend of bears and the guest of eagles. I am Ringwinner and Luckwearer; and I am Barrel-rider," went on Bilbo beginning to be pleased with his riddling.

"That's better!" said Smaug. "But don't let your imagination run away with you!"

This of course is the way to talk to dragons, if you don't want to reveal your proper name (which is wise), and don't want to infuriate them by a flat refusal (which is also very wise). No dragon can resist the fascination of riddling talk and of wasting time trying to understand it. There was a lot here which Smaug did not understand at all, but he thought he understood enough, and he chuckled in his wicked inside.

"I thought so last night," he smiled to himself, "Lake-men, some nasty scheme of those miserable tub-trading Lake-men, or I'm a lizard. I haven't been down that way for an age and an age; but I will soon alter that!"

"Very well, O Barrel-rider!" he said aloud. "Maybe Barrel was your pony's name; and maybe not, though it was fat enough. You may walk unseen, but you did not walk all the way. Let me tell you I ate six ponies last night and I shall catch and eat all the others before long. In return for the excellent meal I will give you one piece of advice for your good: don't have more to do with dwarves than you can help!"

"Dwarves!" said Bilbo in pretended surprise.

"Don't talk to me!" said Smaug. "I know the smell (and taste) of dwarf—no one better. Don't tell me that I can eat a dwarf-ridden pony and not know it! You'll come to a bad end, if you go with such friends, Thief Barrel-rider. I don't mind if you go back and tell them so from me." But he did not tell Bilbo that there was one smell he could not make out at all, hobbit-smell; it was quite outside his experience and puzzled him mightily.

"I suppose you got a fair price for the cup last night?" he went on. "Come now, did you? Nothing at all! Well, that's just like them. And I suppose they are skulking outside, and your job is to do all the dangerous work and get what you can when I'm not looking—for them! And you will get a fair share? Don't you believe it! If you get off alive, you will be lucky."

Bilbo was now beginning to feel really uncomfortable. Whenever Smaug's roving eye, seeking for him in the shadows, flashed across him, he trembled, and an unaccountable desire seized hold of him to rush out and reveal himself and tell all the truth to Smaug. In fact he was in grievous danger of coming under the dragon-spell. But plucking up courage he spoke again.

"You don't know everything, O Smaug the Mighty," said he. "Not gold alone brought us hither."

"Ha! Ha! You admit the 'us'" laughed Smaug. "Why not say 'us fourteen' and be done with it, Mr. Lucky Number? I am pleased to hear that you had other business in these parts besides my gold. In that case you may, perhaps, not altogether waste your time.

"I don't know if it has occurred to you that, even if you could steal the gold bit by bit—a matter of a hundred years or so—you could not get it very far? Not much use on the mountain side? Not much use in the forest? Bless me! Had you never thought of the catch? A fourteenth share, I suppose, or something like it, those were the terms, eh? But what about delivery? What about cartage? What about armed guards and tolls?" And Smaug laughed aloud. He had a wicked and a wily heart, and he knew his guesses were not far out, though he suspected that the Lake-men were at the back of the plans, and that most of the plunder was meant to stop there in the town by the shore that in his young days had been called Esgaroth.

You will hardly believe it, but poor Bilbo was really very taken aback. So far all his thoughts and energies had been concentrated on getting to the Mountain and finding the entrance. He had never bothered to wonder how the treasure was to be removed, certainly never how any part of it that might fall to his share was to be brought back all the way to Bag-End Under-Hill.

Now a nasty suspicion began to grow in his mind—had the dwarves forgotten this important point too, or were they laughing in their sleeves at him all the time? That is the effect that dragon-talk has on the inexperienced. Bilbo of course ought to have been on his guard; but Smaug had rather an overwhelming personality.

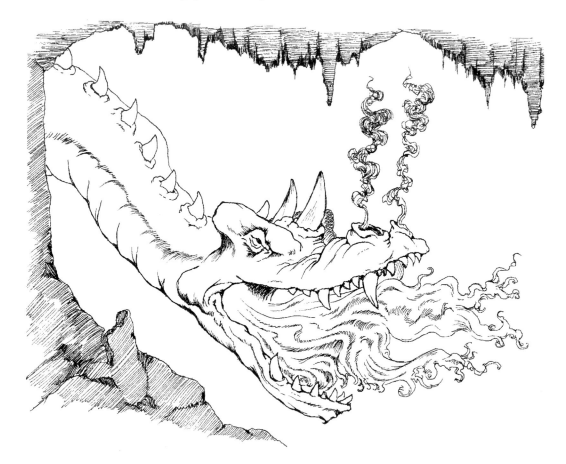

"I tell you," he said, in an effort to remain loyal to his friends and to keep his end up, "that gold was only an afterthought with us. We came over hill and under hill, by wave and wind, for *Revenge*. Surely, O Smaug the unassessably wealthy, you must realize that your success has made you some bitter enemies?"

Then Smaug really did laugh—a devastating sound which shook Bilbo to the floor, while far up in the tunnel the dwarves huddled together and imagined that the hobbit had come to a sudden and a nasty end.

"Revenge!" he snorted, and the light of his eyes lit the hall from floor to ceiling like scarlet lightning. "Revenge! The King under the Mountain is dead and where are his kin that dare seek revenge? Girion Lord of Dale is dead, and I have eaten his people like a wolf among sheep, and where are his sons' sons that dare approach me? I kill where I wish and none dare resist. I laid low the warriors of old and their like is not in the world today. Then I was but young and tender. Now I am old and strong, strong, strong, Thief in the Shadows!" he gloated. "My armor is like tenfold shields, my teeth are swords, my claws spears, the shock of my tail a thunderbolt, my wings a hurricane, and my breath death!"

"I have always understood," said Bilbo in a frightened squeak, "that dragons were softer underneath, especially in the region of the—er—chest; but doubtless one so fortified has thought of that."

The dragon stopped short in his boasting. "Your information is antiquated," he snapped. "I am armored above and below with iron scales and hard gems. No blade can pierce me."

"I might have guessed it," said Bilbo. "Truly there can nowhere be found the equal of Lord Smaug the Impenetrable. What magnificence to possess a waistcoat of fine diamonds!"

"Yes, it is rare and wonderful, indeed," said Smaug absurdly pleased. He did not know that the hobbit had already caught a glimpse of his peculiar undercovering on his previous visit, and was itching for a closer view for reasons of his own. The dragon rolled over. "Look!" he said. "What do you say to that?"

"Dazzlingly marvelous! Perfect! Flawless! Staggering!" exclaimed Bilbo aloud, but what he thought inside was: "Old fool! Why there is a large patch in the hollow of his left breast as bare as a snail out of its shell!"

After he had seen that Mr. Baggins' one idea was to get away. "Well, I really must not detain Your Magnificence any longer," he said, "or keep you from much-needed rest. Ponies take some catching, I believe, after a long start. And so do burglars," he added as a parting shot, as he darted back and fled up the tunnel.

It was an unfortunate remark, for the dragon spouted terrific flames after him, and fast though he sped up the slope, he had not gone nearly far enough to be comfortable before the ghastly head of Smaug was thrust against the opening behind. Luckily the whole head and jaws could not squeeze in, but the nostrils sent forth fire and vapor to pursue him, and he was nearly overcome, and stumbled blindly on in great pain and fear. He had been feeling rather pleased with the cleverness of his conversation with Smaug, but his mistake at the end shook him into better sense.

"Never laugh at live dragons, Bilbo you fool!" he said to himself, and it became a favorite saying of his later, and passed into a proverb. "You aren't nearly through this adventure yet," he added, and that was pretty true as well.

Uncle Lubin
and the Dragon

by W. Heath Robinson

ONLY ONCE IN the course of his travels did Uncle Lubin become really frightened. In a lonely place and during an awful thunderstorm he suddenly came across a dragon-snake which as you will see from the picture is not by any means a pretty thing to meet. Poor Uncle Lubin shivered in his shoes at the sight of this fearful beast, and he made sure that it would fall upon him and eat him up at once, for besides looking ugly it appeared to be very hungry.

After a little while, however, Uncle Lubin's courage returned. He remembered to have heard that when you meet a snake, or for that matter a dragon-snake, the best thing to do is to charm it with music. Fortunately

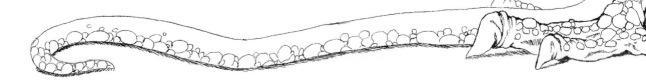

Uncle Lubin had with him his old concertina. On this he at once began to play some beautiful tunes.

The dragon-snake was quite pleased with Uncle Lubin's playing and began to dance to it. Indeed, the snake danced and danced all night through, and by morning it had danced itself into such a tangle, and tied itself into so many knots that it died. Playing the concertina all night tired Uncle Lubin very much, but he was quite glad to have saved his life once again.

The Deliverers of Their Country

by E. Nesbit

I T ALL BEGAN with Effie's getting something in her eye. It hurt very much indeed, and it felt something like a red-hot spark—only it seemed to have legs as well, and wings like a fly. Effie rubbed and cried—not real crying, but the kind your eye does all by itself without your being miserable inside your mind—and then she went to her father to have the thing in her eye taken out.

Effie's father was a doctor, so of course he knew how to take things out of eyes—he did it very cleverly with a soft paintbrush dipped in castor oil. When he had got the thing out, he said, "This is very curious."

Effie had often got things in her eye before, and her father had always seemed to think it was natural—rather tiresome and naughty perhaps, but still natural. He had never before thought it curious. She stood holding her handkerchief to her eye, and said, "I don't believe it's out." People always say this when they have had something in their eye.

"Oh, yes—it's *out*," said the doctor. "Here it is on the brush. This is very interesting."

Effie had never heard her father say that about anything that she had any share in. She said, "*What?*"

The doctor carried the brush very carefully across the room and held the point of it under his microscope. Then he twisted the brass screws of the microscope and looked through the top with one eye.

"Dear me," he said. "Dear, *dear* me! Four well-developed limbs, a long caudal appendage, five toes, unequal in length. Almost like one of the Lacertidae, yet there are traces of wings." The creature under his eye wriggled a little in the castor oil, and he went on: "Yes; a batlike wing. A new specimen, undoubtedly. Effie, run round to the professor and ask him to be kind enough to step in for a few minutes."

"You might give me sixpence, Daddy," said Effie, "because I did bring you the new specimen. I took great care of it inside my eye, and my eye *does* hurt."

The doctor was so pleased with the new specimen that he gave Effie a shilling, and presently the professor stepped round. He stayed to lunch, and he and the doctor quarreled very happily all the afternoon about the name and the family of the thing that had come out of Effie's eye.

But at teatime another thing happened. Effie's brother Harry fished something out of his tea, which he thought at first was an earwig. He was just getting ready to drop it on the floor, and end its life in the usual way, when it shook itself in the spoon—spread two wet wings, and flopped on to the tablecloth. There it sat stroking itself with its feet and stretching its wings, and Harry said, "Why, it's a tiny newt!"

The professor leaned forward before the doctor could say a word. "I'll give you a half a crown for it, Harry, my lad," he said, speaking very fast, and then he picked it up carefully on his handkerchief.

"It is a new specimen," he said, "and finer than yours, doctor."

It was a tiny lizard, about half an inch long—with scales and wings.

So now the doctor and the professor each had a specimen, and they were both very pleased. But before long these specimens began to seem less valuable. For the next morning, when the knife-boy was cleaning the doctor's boots, he suddenly dropped the brushes and the boot and the blacking, and screamed out that he was burned.

And from inside the boot came crawling a lizard as big as a kitten, with large, shiny wings.

"Why," said Effie, "I know what it is. It is a dragon like St. George killed."

And Effie was right. That afternoon Towser was bitten in the garden by a dragon about the size of a rabbit, which he had tried to chase, and next morning all the papers were full of the wonderful "winged lizards" that were appearing all over the country. The papers would not call them dragons, because, of course, no one believes in dragons nowadays—and at any rate the papers were not going to be so silly as to believe in fairy stories. At first there were only a few, but in a week or two the country was simply running alive with dragons of all sizes, and in the air you could sometimes see them as thick as a swarm of bees. They all looked alike except as to size. They were green with scales, and they had four legs and a long tail and great wings like bats' wings, only the wings were a pale, half-transparent yellow, like the gear cases on bicycles.

And they breathed fire and smoke, as all proper dragons must, but still the newspapers went on pretending they were lizards, until the editor of *The Standard* was picked up and carried away by a very large one, and then the other newspaper people had not anyone left to tell them what they ought not to believe. So that when the largest elephant in the zoo was carried off by a dragon, the papers gave up pretending—and put ALARMING PLAGUE OF DRAGONS at the top of the paper.

And you have no idea how alarming it was, and at the same time how aggravating. The large-sized dragons were terrible certainly, but when once you had found out that the dragons always went to bed early because they were afraid of the chill night air, you had only to stay indoors all day, and you were pretty safe from the big ones.

But the smaller sizes were a perfect nuisance. The ones as big as earwigs got in the soap, and they got in the butter. The ones as big as dogs got in the bath, and the fire and smoke inside them made them steam like anything when the cold water tap was turned on, so that careless people were often scalded quite severely. The ones that were as large as pigeons would get into workbaskets or corner drawers, and bite you when you were in a hurry to get a needle or a handkerchief.

The ones as big as sheep were easier to avoid, because you could see them coming, but when they flew in at the windows and curled up under your eiderdown, and you did not find them till you went to bed, it was always a shock. The ones this size did not eat people, only lettuces, but they always scorched the sheets and pillowcases dreadfully.

Of course the county council and the police did everything that could be done. It was no use offering the hand of the princess to anyone who killed a dragon. This way was all very well in olden times—when there was only one dragon and one princess, but now there were far more dragons than princesses—although the royal family was a large one. And besides, it would have been mere waste of princesses to offer rewards for killing dragons, because everybody killed as many dragons as they could quite out of their own heads and without rewards at all, just to get the nasty things out of the way. The county council undertook to cremate all dragons delivered at their offices between the hours of ten and two, and whole wagonloads and cartloads and truckloads of dead dragons could be seen any day of the week standing in a long line in the street where the county council lived. Boys brought barrowloads of dead dragons, and children on their way home from morning school would call in to leave the handful or two of little dragons they had brought in their satchels, or carried in their knotted pocket handkerchiefs. And yet there seemed to be as many dragons as ever. Then the police stuck up great wood and canvas towers covered with patent glue. When the dragons flew against these towers, they stuck fast, as flies and wasps do on the sticky papers in the kitchen, and when the towers were covered all over with dragons, the police inspector used to set light to the towers, and burned them and dragons and all.

And yet there seemed to be more dragons than ever. The shops were full of patent dragon poison and antidragon soap, and dragonproof curtains for the windows. And indeed, everything that could be done was done.

And yet there seemed to be more dragons than ever.

It was not very easy to know what would poison a dragon, because you see they ate such different things. The largest kind ate elephants as long as there were any, and then went on with horses and cows. Another size ate nothing but lilies of the valley, and a third size ate only prime ministers if they were to be had, and if not, would feed freely on boys in buttons. Another size lived on bricks, and three of them ate two-thirds of the South Lambeth Infirmary in one afternoon.

But the size Effie was most afraid of was about as big as your dining room, and that size ate *little girls and boys.*

At first Effie and her brother were quite pleased with the change in their lives. It was so amusing to sit up all night instead of going to sleep, and to play in the garden lighted by electric lamps.

And it sounded so funny to hear mother say, when they were going to bed, "Good night, my darlings, sleep sound all day, and don't get up too soon. You must not get up before it's *quite* dark. You wouldn't like the nasty dragons to catch you."

But after a time they got very tired of it all: they wanted to see the flowers and trees growing in the fields, and to see the pretty sunshine out of doors, and not just through glass windows and patent dragonproof curtains. And they wanted to play on the grass, which they were not allowed to do in the electric-lamp-lighted garden because of the night dew.

And they wanted so much to get out, just for once, in the beautiful, bright, dangerous daylight, that they began to try and think of some reason why they *ought* to go out. Only they did not like to disobey their mother.

But one morning their mother was busy preparing some new dragon poison to lay down in the cellars, and their father was bandaging the hand of the bootboy which had been scratched by one of the dragons who liked to eat prime ministers when they were to be had, so nobody remembered to say to the children "Don't get up till it is quite dark!"

"Go now," said Harry. "It would not be disobedient to go. And I know exactly what we ought to do, but I don't know how we ought to do it."

"What ought we do?" said Effie.

"We ought to wake St. George, of course," said Harry. "He was the only person in his town who knew how to manage dragons—the people in the fairy tales don't count. But St. George is a real person, and he is only asleep, and he is waiting to be waked up. Only nobody believes in St. George now. I heard father say so."

"*We* do," said Effie.

"Of course we do. And don't you see, Ef, that's the very reason why we could wake him? You can't wake people if you don't believe in them, can you?"

Effie said no, but where could they find St. George?

"We must go and look," said Harry boldly. "You shall wear a dragon-proof frock, made of stuff like the curtains. And I will smear myself all over with the best dragon poison, and—"

Effie clasped her hands and skipped with joy, and cried, "Oh, Harry! I know where we can find St. George! In St. George's Church, of course."

"Um," said Harry, wishing he had thought of it for himself, "you have a little sense sometimes, for a girl."

So next afternoon quite early, long before the beams of sunset announced the coming night, when everybody would be up and working, the two children got out of bed. Effie wrapped herself in a shawl of dragon-proof muslin—there was no time to make the frock—and Harry made a horrid mess of himself with the patent dragon poison. It was warranted harmless to infants and invalids, so he felt quite safe.

Then they took hands and set out to walk to St. George's Church. As you know, there are many St. George's churches but fortunately they took the turning that leads to the right one, and went along in the bright sunlight, feeling very brave and adventurous.

There was no one about in the streets except dragons, and the place was simply swarming with them. Fortunately none of the dragons were just the right size for eating little boys and girls, or perhaps this story might have had to end here. There were dragons on the pavement, and dragons on the roadway, dragons basking on the front doorsteps of public buildings, and dragons preening their wings on the roofs in the hot afternoon sun. The town was quite green with them. Even when the children had got out of the town and were walking in the lanes, they noticed that the fields on each side were greener than usual with the scaly legs and tails, and some of the smaller sizes had made themselves asbestos nests in the flowering hawthorn hedges.

Effie held her brother's hand very tightly, and once when a fat dragon flopped against her ear she screamed out, and a whole flight of green dragons rose from the field at the sound, and sprawled away across the sky. The children could hear the rattle of their wings as they flew.

"Oh, I want to go home," said Effie.

"Don't be silly," said Harry. "Surely you haven't forgotten about the Seven Champions* and all the princes. People who are going to be their country's deliverers never scream and say they want to go home."

"And are we?" asked Effie. "Deliverers, I mean?"

"You'll see," said her brother, and on they went.

When they came to St. George's Church they found the door open, and they walked right in—but St. George was not there, so they walked round the churchyard outside, and presently they found the great stone tomb of St. George, with the figure of him carved in marble outside, in his armor and helmet, and with his hands folded on his breast.

"How ever can we wake him?" they said.

Then Harry spoke to St. George—but he would not answer. And he called, but St. George did not seem to hear. And then he actually tried to waken the great dragon slayer by shaking his marble shoulders. But St. George took no notice.

Then Effie began to cry, and she put her arms round St. George's neck as well as she could for the marble, which was very much in the way at the back, and she kissed the marble face, and she said, "Oh, dear, good, kind St. George, please wake up and help us."

And at that St. George opened his eyes sleepily, and stretched himself and said, "What's the matter, little girl?"

So the children told him all about it. He turned over in his marble and

*The patron saints of England, Scotland, Wales, Ireland, France, Italy, and Spain.

leaned on one elbow to listen. But when he heard that there were so many dragons he shook his head.

"It's no good," he said. "They would be one too many for poor old George. You should have wakened me before. I was always for a fair fight— one man one dragon was my motto."

Just then a flight of dragons passed overhead, and St. George half drew his sword.

But he shook his head again and pushed the sword back as the flight of dragons grew small in the distance.

"I can't do anything," he said. "Things have changed since my time. St. Andrew told me about it. They woke him up over the engineers' strike, and he came to talk to me. He says everything is done by machinery now. There must be some way of settling these dragons. By the way, what sort of weather have you been having lately?"

This seemed so careless and unkind that Harry could not answer, but Effie said, patiently, "It has been very fine. Father says it is the hottest weather there has ever been in this country."

"Ah, I guessed as much," said the champion thoughtfully. "Well, the only thing would be…dragons can't stand wet and cold, that's the only thing. If you could find the taps."

St. George was beginning to settle down again on his stone slab.

"Good night, very sorry I can't help you," he said, yawning behind his marble hand.

"Oh, but you can," cried Effie. "Tell us—what taps?"

"Oh, like in the bathroom," said St. George, still more sleepily. "And there's a looking glass, too. Shows you all the world and what's going on. St. Denis told me about it. Said it was a very pretty thing. I'm sorry I can't—good night."

And he fell back into his marble and was fast asleep again in a moment.

"We shall never find the taps," said Harry. "I say, wouldn't it be awful if St. George woke up when there was a dragon near, the size that eats champions?"

Effie pulled off her dragonproof veil. "We didn't meet any the size of the dining room as we came along," she said. "I daresay we shall be quite safe."

So she covered St. George with the veil, and Harry rubbed off as much as he could of the dragon poison onto St. George's armor, so as to make everything quite safe for him.

"We might hide in the church till it is dark," he said, "and then—"

But at that moment a dark shadow fell on them, and they saw that it was a dragon exactly the size of the dining room at home.

So then they knew that all was lost. The dragon swooped down and caught the two children in his claws. He caught Effie by her green silk sash and Harry by the little point at the back of his Eton jacket—and then, spreading his great yellow wings, he rose into the air, rattling like a third-class carriage when the brake is hard on.

"Oh, Harry," said Effie, "I wonder when he will eat us!" The dragon was flying across woods and fields with great flaps of his wings that carried him a quarter of a mile at each flap.

Harry and Effie could see the country below, hedges and rivers and churches and farmhouses flowing away from under them, much faster than you see them running away from the sides of the fastest express train.

And still the dragon flew on. The children saw other dragons in the air as they went, but the dragon who was as big as the dining room never stopped to speak to any of them, but just flew on quite steadily.

"He knows where he wants to go," said Harry. "Oh, if he would only drop us before he gets there!"

But the dragon held on tight, and he flew and flew and flew until at

last, when the children were quite giddy, he settled down, with a rattling of all his scales, on the top of a mountain. And he lay there on his great green scaly side, panting, and very much out of breath, because he had come such a long way. But his claws were fast in Effie's sash and the little point at the back of Harry's Eton jacket.

Then Effie took out the knife Harry had given her on her birthday. It only cost sixpence to begin with, and she had had it a month, and it never could sharpen anything but slate pencils, but somehow she managed to make that knife cut her sash in front, and crept out of it, leaving the dragon with only a green silk bow in one of his claws. That knife would never have cut Harry's jacket tail off, though, and when Effie had tried for some time she saw that this was so, and gave it up. But with her help Harry managed to wriggle quietly out of his sleeves, so that the dragon had only an Eton jacket in his other claw.

Then the children crept on tiptoe to a crack in the rocks and got in. It was much too narrow for the dragon to get in also, so they stayed in there and waited to make faces at the dragon when he felt rested enough to sit up and begin to think about eating them. He was very angry, indeed, when they made faces at him, and blew out fire and smoke at them but they ran farther into the cave so that he could not reach them, and when he was tired of blowing he went away.

But they were afraid to come out of the cave, so they went farther in and presently the cave opened out and grew bigger, and the floor was soft sand, and when they had come to the very end of the cave there was a door, and on it was written:

UNIVERSAL TAPROOM

PRIVATE

NO ONE ALLOWED INSIDE

So they opened the door at once just to peep in, and then they remembered what St. George had said.

"We can't be worse off than we are," said Harry, "with a dragon waiting for us outside. Let's go in."

So they went boldly into the taproom and shut the door behind them.

And now they were in a sort of room cut out of the solid rock, and all along one side of the room were taps, and all the taps were labeled with china labels like you see in baths. And as they could both read words of two syllables or even three sometimes, they understood at once that they had got to the place where the weather is turned on from.

There were six big taps labeled "Sunshine," "Wind," "Rain," "Snow," "Hail," "Ice," and a lot of little ones labeled "Fair to moderate," "Showery," "South breeze," "Nice growing weather for the crops," "Skating," "Good open weather," "South wind," "East wind," and so on.

And the big tap labeled "Sunshine" was turned full on. They could not see any sunshine—the cave was lighted by a skylight of blue glass—so they supposed the sunlight was pouring out by some other way, as it does with the tap that washes out the underneath parts of patent sinks in kitchens.

Then they saw that one side of the room was just a big looking glass, and when you looked in it you could see everything that was going on in the world—and all at once, too, which is not like most looking glasses. They saw the carts delivering the dead dragons at the county council offices, and they saw St. George asleep under the dragonproof veil. And they saw their mother at home crying because her children had gone out in the dreadful, dangerous daylight, and she was afraid a dragon had eaten them.

And they saw the whole of England, like a great puzzle map—green in the field parts and brown in the towns, and black in the places where they make coal, and crockery, and cutlery, and chemicals. And all over it, on the black parts, and on the brown, and on the green, there was a network of green dragons. And they could see that it was still broad daylight, and no dragons had gone to bed yet.

So Effie said, "Dragons do not like cold." And she tried to turn off the sunshine, but the tap was out of order, and that was why there had been so much hot weather, and why the dragons had been able to be hatched. So they left the sunshine tap alone, and they turned on the snow and left the tap full on while they went to look in the glass. There they saw the dragons running all sorts of ways like ants if you are cruel enough to pour water into an ant heap, which, of course, you never are. And the snow fell more and more.

Then Effie turned the rain tap quite full on, and presently the dragons began to wriggle less, and by and by some of them lay quite still, so the children knew the water had put out the fires inside them, and they were dead. So then they turned on the hail—only half on, for fear of breaking people's windows—and after a while there were no more dragons to be seen moving.

Then the children knew that they were indeed the deliverers of their country.

"They will put up a monument to us," said Harry, "as high as Nelson's! All the dragons are dead."

"I hope the one that was waiting outside for us is dead!" said Effie. "And about the monument, Harry, I'm not so sure. What can they do with such a lot of dead dragons? It would take years and years to bury them, and they could never be burned now they are so soaking wet. I wish the rain would wash them off into the sea."

But this did not happen, and the children began to feel that they had not been so frightfully clever after all.

"I wonder what this old thing's for," said Harry. He had found a rusty old tap, which seemed as though it had not been used for ages. Its china label was quite coated over with dirt and cobwebs. When Effie had cleaned it with a bit of her skirt—for curiously enough both the children had come out without pocket handkerchiefs—she found that the label said "Waste."

"Let's turn it on," she said. "It might carry off the dragons."

The tap was very stiff from not having been used for such a long time, but together they managed to turn it on, and then ran to the mirror to see what happened.

Already a great, round, black hole had opened in the very middle of the map of England, and the sides of the map were tilting themselves up, so that the rain ran down towards the hole.

"Oh, hurrah, hurrah, hurrah!" cried Effie, and she hurried back to the taps and turned on everything that seemed wet. "Showery," "Good open weather," "Nice growing weather for the crops," and even "South" and "Southwest," because she had heard her father say that those winds brought rain.

And now the floods of rain were pouring down on the country, and great sheets of water flowed towards the center of the map, and cataracts of water poured into the great round hole in the middle of the map, and the dragons were being washed away and disappearing down the waste pipe in great green masses and scattered green shoals—single dragons and dragons by the dozen; of all sizes, from the ones that carry off elephants down to the ones that get in your tea.

And presently there was not a dragon left. So then they turned off the tap named "Waste," and they half-turned off the one labeled "Sunshine"—it was broken, so that they could not turn it off altogether—and they turned on "Fair to moderate" and "Showery" and both taps stuck, so that they could not be turned off, which accounts for our climate.

How did they get home again? By the Snowdon railway—of course.

And was the nation grateful? Well—the nation was very wet. And by the time the nation had got dry again it was interested in the new invention for toasting muffins by electricity, and all the dragons were almost forgotten. Dragons do not seem so important when they are dead and gone, and you know there never was a reward offered.

And what did father and mother say when Effie and Harry got home?

My dear, that is the sort of silly question you children always will ask. However, just for this once I don't mind telling you.

Mother said, "Oh, my darlings, my darlings, you're safe—you're safe! You naughty children—how could you be so disobedient? Go to bed at once!"

And their father the doctor said, "I wish I had known what you were going to do! I should have liked to preserve a specimen. I threw away the one I got out of Effie's eye. I intended to get a more perfect specimen. I did not anticipate this immediate extinction of the species."

The professor said nothing, but he rubbed his hands. He had kept his specimen—the one the size of an earwig that he gave Harry half a crown for—and he has it to this day.

You must get him to show it to you!

The Devil and His Grandmother

by the Brothers Grimm

THERE WAS A great war, and the King had many soldiers, but gave them small pay, so small that they could not live upon it, so three of them agreed among themselves to desert. One of them said to the others: "If we are caught we shall be hanged on the gallows; how shall we manage it?" Another said: "Look at the great cornfield, if we were to hide ourselves there, no one could find us; the troops are not allowed to enter it, and tomorrow they are to march away." They crept into the corn, only the troops did not march away, but remained lying all round about it.

They stayed in the corn for two days and two nights, and were so hungry that they all but died, but if they had come out, their death would have

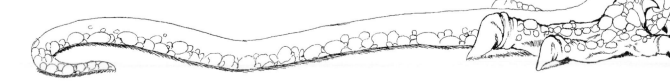

been certain. Then said they: "What is the use of our deserting if we have to perish miserably here?" But now a fiery dragon came flying through the air, and it came down to them, and asked why they had concealed themselves there. They answered: "We are three soldiers who have deserted because the pay was so bad, and now we shall have to die of hunger if we stay here, or to dangle on the gallows if we go out."

"If you will serve me for seven years," said the dragon, "I will convey you through the army so that no one shall seize you."

"We have no choice and are compelled to accept," they replied.

Then the dragon caught hold of them with his claws, and carried them away through the air over the army, and put them down again on the earth far from it; but the dragon was no other than the Devil. He gave them a small whip and said: "Whip with it and crack it, and then as much gold will spring up round about as you can wish for; then you can live like great lords, keep horses, and drive your carriages, but when the seven years have come to an end, you are my property." Then he put before them a book which they were all three forced to sign. "But first I will ask you a riddle," said he, "and if you can guess it, you shall be free, and released from my power."

Then the dragon flew away from them, and they went away with their whip, had gold in plenty, ordered themselves rich apparel, and traveled about the world. Wherever they were they lived in pleasure and magnificence, rode on horseback, drove in carriages, ate and drank, but did nothing wicked. The time slipped quickly by, and when the seven years were coming to an end, two of them were terribly anxious and alarmed; but the third took the affair easily, and said: "Brothers, fear nothing, I still have my wits about me, I shall guess the riddle." They went out into the open country and sat down, and the two pulled sorrowful faces.

Then an aged woman came up to them who inquired why they were so sad. "Well," said they, "what has that got to do with you? After all, you cannot help us."

"Who knows?" said she, "just confide your trouble to me." So they told her that they had been the Devil's servants for nearly seven years, and that he had provided them with gold as though it were hay, but that they had sold themselves to him, and were forfeited to him, if at the end of the seven years they could not guess a riddle. The old woman said: "If you are to be saved, one of you must go into the forest, there he will come to a fallen rock which looks like a little house, he must enter that, and then he will obtain help."

The two melancholy ones thought to themselves: "That will still not save us," and stayed where they were, but the third, the merry one, got up and walked on in the forest until he found the rock-house. In the little house a very aged woman was sitting, who was the Devil's grandmother, and asked the soldier where he came from, and what he wanted there.

He told her everything that had happened, and as he pleased her well, she had pity on him, and said she would help him. She lifted up a great stone which lay above a cellar, and said: "Conceal yourself there, you can hear everything that is said here; only sit still, and do not stir. When the dragon comes, I will question him about the riddle, he tells everything to me, so listen carefully to his answer."

At twelve o'clock at night, the dragon came flying thither, and asked for his dinner. The grandmother laid the table, and served up food and drink, so that he was pleased, and they ate and drank together. In the course of conversation, she asked him what kind of a day he had had, and how many souls he had got. "Nothing went very well today," he answered, "but I have laid hold of three soldiers—I have them safe."

"Indeed! Three soldiers, they're clever, they may escape you yet."

The Devil said mockingly: "They are mine! I will set them a riddle, which they will never be able to guess!"

"What riddle is that?" she inquired.

"I will tell you: in the great North Sea lies a dead dogfish, that shall be your roast meat, and the rib of a whale shall be your silver spoon, and a hollow old horse's hoof shall be your wineglass."

When the Devil had gone to bed, the old grandmother raised up the stone, and let out the soldier. "Did you give heed to everything?"

"Yes," said he, "I know enough, and will save myself." Then he had to go back another way, through the window, secretly and with all speed to his companions. He told them how the Devil had been outwitted by the old grandmother, and how he had learned the answer to the riddle from him. Then they were all delighted, and of good cheer, and took the whip and whipped so much gold for themselves that it ran all over the ground.

When the seven years had fully gone by, the Devil came with the book, showed the signatures, and said: "I will take you with me to hell. There you shall have a meal! If you can guess what kind of roast meat you will have to eat, you shall be free and released from your bargain, and may keep the whip as well."

Then the first soldier began and said: "In the great North Sea lies a dead dogfish, that no doubt is the roast meat."

The Devil was angry, and began to mutter "Hm! Hm! Hm!" and asked the second: "But what will your spoon be?"

"The rib of a whale, that is to be our silver spoon."

The Devil made a wry face, again growled "Hm! Hm! Hm!" and said to the third: "And do you also know what your wineglass is to be?"

"An old horse's hoof is to be our wineglass."

Then the Devil flew away with a loud cry, and had no more power over them, but the three kept the whip, whipped as much money for themselves with it as they wanted, and lived happily to their end.

Sigurd and Fafnir

retold by Andrew Lang

ONCE UPON A time there was a King in the North who had won many wars, but now he was old. Yet he took a new wife, and then another Prince, who wanted to have married her, came up against him with a great army. The old King went out and fought bravely, but alas his sword broke, and he was wounded and his men fled. But in the night, when the battle was over, his young wife came out and searched for him among the slain, and at last she found him, and asked whether he might be healed. But he said "No," his luck was gone, his sword was broken, and he must die. And he told her that she would have a son, and that son would be a great warrior, and would avenge him on the other King, his enemy. And he bade her keep the broken pieces of the sword, to make a new sword for his son, and that blade should be called *Gram.*

Then he died. And his wife called her maid to her and said, "Let us change clothes, and you shall be called by my name, and I by yours, lest the enemy finds us."

So this was done, and they hid in a wood, but there some strangers met them and carried them off in a ship to Denmark. And when they were brought before the King, he thought the maid looked like a Queen, and the Queen like a maid. So he asked the Queen, "How do you know in the dark of night whether the hours are wearing to the morning?"

And she said:

"I know because, when I was younger, I used to have to rise and light the fires, and still I waken at the same time."

"A strange Queen to light the fires," thought the King.

Then he asked the Queen, who was dressed like a maid, "How do you know in the dark of night whether the hours are wearing near the dawn?"

"My father gave me a gold ring," said she, "and always, ere the dawning, it grows cold on my finger."

"A rich house where the maids wore gold," said the King. "Truly you are no maid, but a King's daughter."

So he treated her royally, and as time went on she had a son called Sigurd, a beautiful boy and very strong. He had a tutor to be with him, and once the tutor bade him go to the King and ask for a horse.

"Choose a horse for yourself," said the King; and Sigurd went to the wood, and there he met an old man with a white beard, and said, "Come! Help me in horse-choosing."

Then the old man said, "Drive all the horses into the river, and choose the one that swims across."

So Sigurd drove them, and only one swam across. Sigurd chose him: his name was Grani, and he came of Sleipnir's breed, and was the best horse in the world. For Sleipnir was the horse of Odin, the God of the North, and was as swift as the wind.

But a day or two later his tutor said to Sigurd, "There is a great treasure of gold hidden not far from here, and it would become you to win it."

But Sigurd answered, "I have heard stories of that treasure, and I know that the dragon Fafnir guards it, and he is so huge and wicked that no man dares to go near him."

"He is no bigger than other dragons," said the tutor, "and if you were as brave as your father you would not fear him."

"I am no coward," says Sigurd; "why do you want me to fight with this dragon?"

Then his tutor, whose name was Regin, told him that all this great hoard of red gold had once belonged to his own father. And his father had three sons—the first was Fafnir, the Dragon; the next was Otter, who could put on the shape of an otter when he liked; and the next was himself, Regin, and he was a great smith and maker of swords.

Now there was at that time a dwarf called Andvari, who lived in a pool beneath a waterfall, and there he had hidden a great hoard of gold. And one day Otter had been fishing there, and had killed a salmon and eaten it, and was sleeping, like an otter, on a stone. Then someone came by, and threw a stone at the otter and killed it, and flayed off the skin, and took it to the house of Otter's father. Then he knew his son was dead, and to punish the person who had killed him he said he must have the otter's skin filled with gold, and covered all over with red gold, or it should go worse with him. Then the person who had killed Otter went down and caught the Dwarf who owned all the treasure and took it from him.

Only one ring was left, which the Dwarf wore, and even that was taken from him.

Then the poor Dwarf was very angry, and he prayed that the gold might never bring any but bad luck to all the men who might own it, for ever.

Then the otter skin was filled with gold and covered with gold, all but one hair, and that was covered with the poor Dwarf's last ring.

But it brought good luck to nobody. First Fafnir, the Dragon, killed his own father, and then he went and wallowed on the gold, and would let his brother have none, and no man dared go near it.

When Sigurd heard the story he said to Regin:

"Make me a good sword that I may kill this Dragon."

So Regin made a sword, and Sigurd tried it with a blow on a lump of iron, and the sword broke.

Another sword he made, and Sigurd broke that too.

Then Sigurd went to his mother, and asked for the broken pieces of his father's blade, and gave them to Regin. And he hammered and wrought them into a new sword, so sharp that fire seemed to burn along its edges.

Sigurd tried this blade on the lump of iron, and it did not break, but split the iron in two. Then he threw a lock of wool into the river, and when it floated down against the sword it was cut into two pieces. So Sigurd said that sword would do. But before he went against the Dragon he led an army to fight the men who had killed his father, and he slew their King, and took all his wealth, and went home.

When he had been at home a few days, he rode out with Regin one morning to the heath where the Dragon used to lie. Then he saw the track which the Dragon made when he went to a cliff to drink, and the track was as if a great river had rolled along and left a deep valley.

Then Sigurd went down into that deep place, and dug many pits in it, and in one of the pits he lay hidden with his sword drawn. There he waited, and presently the earth began to shake with the weight of the Dragon as he crawled to the water. And a cloud of venom flew before him as he snorted and roared, so that it would have been death to stand before him.

But Sigurd waited till half of him had crawled over the pit, and then he thrust the sword Gram right into his very heart.

Then the Dragon lashed with his tail till stones broke and trees crashed about him.

Then he spoke, as he died, and said:

"Whoever thou art that hast slain me this gold shall be thy ruin, and the ruin of all who own it."

Sigurd said:

"I would touch none of it if by losing it I should never die. But all men die, and no brave man lets death frighten him from his desire. Die thou, Fafnir," and then Fafnir died.

And after that Sigurd was called Fafnir's Bane, and Dragonslayer.

The Story of Wang Li

by Elizabeth Coatsworth

ONCE IN CHINA many many years ago there lived a young man named Wang Li, with his old mother, on a small farm under the shadow of the Hill of the Seven Stars. When he was a boy he studied letters and charms with a famous sage who lived by himself in the Wind Cave halfway up the mountain. But when he had studied for several years he declared one morning that he would climb the rough path no more.

His mother was in despair.

"How hard have I labored without your help in the fields!" she cried. "Why, in a few years you could have called the cranes out of the sky to carry us anywhere we wished, or turned flower petals into money to buy whatever we desired! Ungrateful son! Return to your studies!"

But Wang Li only shook his head.

"I have learned all that I need," he replied. *"A big heart is better than a big house."*

Upon hearing a proverb quoted at her, Wang Li's mother grew furious, and seizing her broom, beat Wang Li over the shoulders until she was tired. He, being a filial son in most matters, waited until she had stopped, and then brought her a drink of cold water fresh from the well.

After that Wang Li helped his mother in the fields, but often he slipped away to the forests at the foot of the Hill of the Seven Stars with his bow and arrow, to wander in their green shades and perhaps bring back a hare for their dinner, until he became as expert a hunter as there was in the countryside.

So the days went by and at last there came a dry spring. Week after week passed and still no rain fell and the young rice and millet shoots stood small and yellow in the fields, and the mulberry leaves hung withered on the trees, unfit for the silkworms, and the melon vines lay brittle as straws on the baked ground. Prayers were said all day long in the Temple of the God of the Soil. Incense burned in great twisted ropes of sweetness about his nostrils, gongs were sounded before him, and offerings of fish and chickens and pork lay heaped on his altars.

But still no rain fell.

Early one morning Wang Li was wandering in the forest when he saw something above his head that looked like a flight of great swans, slowly settling down towards the clear waters of Heaven Mirror Lake. Creeping without sound through the underbrush, he at last came to a thicket at the very edge of the water, and parting the leaves with careful hands, he beheld a most beautiful sight. The creatures whom he had seen were not swans but winged maidens who were playing about on the surface, splashing the water until it shone like the crystal beads in their elaborate headdresses, shaking their white wings with a sound like music, clapping their delicate hands, and pursuing one another in sport.

It happened that during their games the most beautiful of the damsels passed close to the thicket where Wang Li was hidden. Swift as a hawk he seized one snow-white wing in his strong hand, and while the other maidens rose screaming into the air, he drew his lovely captive to the shore.

For a little while she wept, but glancing at him through her lashes, she was reassured and ceased to sob. Still holding the edge of one bright wing, he questioned her.

"What is your name, beautiful one?" he asked.

"I am called the Sky Damsel and am the youngest daughter of the Cloud Dragon," she answered timidly. And then went on: "You are the first human being I have ever seen. If you will come with me I will take you to the sixteen palaces of my father that are built upon the clouds. One palace is of white jade and silver, and butterflies guard the gates; another palace is built of marble inlaid with rose quartz, and its gardens are famous for their peonies; another palace has walls of gold, and is overlooked by a high pagoda on which stands the bird of the sun to crow to the dawn; and the last palace is built of ebony with pavilions of scarlet lacquer, and Lightning stands on the left of the gate and Thunder on the right. If you will come, you shall be my husband and live in whichever palace you please, and you shall ride on steeds of vapor and pluck the stars as you pass."

"I am a poor man," said Wang Li, "and the son of a poor man. How should I live in a palace? But if I give you your freedom, Sky Damsel, will you swear to me that in return you will ask your august parent to send upon this unfortunate countryside the requisite rains, so that the crops will flour-

ish and the people may not die? And he might keep a special eye on my mother's little farm at the foot of Seven Stars Hill," he added, "for she works hard and likes her garden to do well."

"It shall be as you have said," replied the Sky Damsel, and she flew away, often looking back and weeping.

But Wang Li returned home, and as he neared his mother's house the rain began to fall, soft and warm, filling all the ditches with the gurgle of running water.

"Rejoice," cried his mother as he entered, "the drought is over! And just in time, too! Now the crops will be spared. I wonder how it occurred?"

"Oh, I know all about *that*," said Wang Li, and he told her what had happened by the lonely shore of Heaven Mirror Lake.

At once his mother flew into a rage.

"And you only asked for rain," she screamed, "when we might have lived in palaces, and worn silk woven from moonlight, and fed on the fruit of the immortals! Oh, you undutiful son!"

And she fell to beating him with her broom. But when at last she stopped exhausted, he only remarked:

"*A chicken coop is still a chicken coop even when covered with a cloth of gold.*" And he lifted a pot of dumplings which was in danger of boiling over.

Now the next year it happened that Roving Horse River was in flood, spreading out over its banks, ruining fields, and carrying away houses. Its waters came up nearly to the door of the cottage where Wang Li and his mother lived, and threatened her mulberry trees. She was in despair and wept bitterly, but Wang Li took his bow and arrow from the wall.

"Are you going hunting at such a time?" she screamed. "Oh, that I should have borne a son with no heart!"

But he only said: "*If you know how, a thing is not hard; if it is hard, then you don't know how.*" And he left her with her mouth open, not understanding what he meant.

"I wish that boy would stop quoting proverbs," she muttered to herself. "He is as clever a boy as ever breathed, but what good does it do us?"

Meantime Wang Li walked along beside the bank of the river. And he saw the flood coming down in a great white wave. And having very keen eyes he saw in the midst of the wave a youth and a maiden, clothed in garments of white silk, riding white horses with silver bits. And attendants on white horses followed them.

Then Wang Li drew his bow, fitted an arrow into the string, and let it fly straight into the heart of the young man, who fell dead from his horse. At that the others turned their horses and rode away at full speed, and the flood receded with them.

But as they rode, Wang Li sent another arrow after them, which pierced the high headdress of the noble lady and shone there like a long ornament. And after a few paces, she reined in her horse and slowly rode back to where Wang Li stood.

"Here is your arrow," she said, giving it to him. "I suppose I should thank you for not sending it through my heart as you did through my cousin's, the Prince of Roving Horse River."

"I could never do anything so discourteous," murmured Wang Li.

The lady regarded him for a long time.

"Since you have spared my person," she said, "I suppose it should be yours. If you will come with me you shall be my husband, and reign in the palaces of the River Dragons. You shall sit on a throne of coral in halls of jade and crystal, and the River Maidens shall dance before you the Dance of the Ripples, and the River Warriors shall dance to please you the Dance of the Tempest."

"And what will happen to the countryside while they dance?" asked Wang Li. "No, no, I am a poor man and the son of a poor man. What should I do in palaces? If you wish to show your gratitude, make me a pledge that the river shall hereafter stay within its banks, and perhaps you might be especially careful along the edge of my mother's farm, for she is a poor woman and it grieves her to see her work washed away."

The lady raised her hand in agreement, and turned her horse, and rode off. But before she disappeared forever, she looked back for a last glimpse of Wang Li, and he saw that she was weeping. A little sad, he returned to his mother's house and, as he walked, he noticed how the waters were draining off the land, leaving behind them, as tribute, pools filled with round-mouthed fish.

His mother met him at the door.

"See! See!" she cried, "the waters are withdrawing! But you, you wicked son, you left me here to drown and little you cared!"

"Indeed, I only went to bring you help!" said Wang Li, and he told his mother all that had happened. At hearing the story she nearly choked with rage.

"What! We might have lived in river palaces and dined off turtle eggs and carps' tongues every day!" she cried. "And I might have ridden on a dragon forty feet long when I went calling! All this might have been mine but you refused it, you ungrateful son!" And she seized her broom.

Whack!

"Take that!"

Whack!

"And that!"

Whack! Whack! Whack!

"And that! And that! And that!"

But when at last her arm fell, Wang Li politely helped her to her chair and brought her a fan.

"Peace in a thatched hut—that is happiness," he said, once more quoting an old proverb.

"Be off with you!" replied his mother. "You are a wicked, ungrateful son and have no right to be using the words of wise men. Besides, they hadn't been offered palaces, I'm sure."

So the months passed and the rain fell when it was needed, and the river remained within its banks and reflected on its smooth waters the sun by day and the moon by night. But after some time the country was greatly disturbed by earthquakes. People were awakened from their sleep by the tremblings of their beds, the dishes danced on the tables, sheds fell flat to the earth, and everyone waited with horror for the final quake that should bring the roofs down on their heads.

"Now," wept Wang Li's old mother, "I shall die a violent death, I who might have slept safe beside the Silver Stream of Heaven or walked in the gardens of the river, if it had not been for this great foolish son."

But Wang Li took his spear and went to the mouth of the Cave of the Evening Sun which is on the west side of the Hills of the Seven Stars. Then he looked carefully at the ground beneath his feet, which was rounded up as though a huge mole had passed under it, and choosing a certain spot, drove his spear deep into the loosened soil.

"Whoever walks along that path again will scratch his back," he said to himself with satisfaction, and was about to return home when he noticed a beautiful girl who sat beside a rock spinning, and weeping as she spun.

"Why do you scatter the pearls of your eyes, young maiden?" asked Wang Li gently. And she, raising her tear-wet eyes to him, said:

"Alas, I am Precious Jade, the only daughter of the former Dragon King of the Mountains. But my ungrateful uncle has risen against his elder brother and imprisoned him in the innermost prison of the hills, and he has driven me out to work with unaccustomed hands, living in this coarse robe, and eating roots and berries, and sleeping under the stars."

Wang Li looked at her in her rough brown garments, and her beauty seemed like a flower bursting from its sheath.

"I think I have stopped the path of your uncle who has been disturbing us with his wanderings, and now perhaps he will stay in his cavern palaces. But for you I can do nothing, I fear, though I would gladly serve you."

At that Precious Jade looked at him shyly.

"If you would deign to take me away with you and allow me to serve your mother with my poor strength, I should no longer weep alone on this desolate mountain," she whispered.

"And what gifts would you bring my mother if I took you home as a bride?" asked Wang Li.

Then Precious Jade wrung her hands. "Alas," she said, "I have no gifts but only my will to serve you both." And she wept very bitterly.

At that Wang Li laughed and lifted her up in his arms and carried her home to his mother.

"Mercy!" cried the old woman, "whom have we here?"

"It is Precious Jade, the daughter of the former Dragon King of the Mountains," said Wang Li, "and she has returned here to be your daughter-in-law."

The old woman was all in a flutter.

"I must have an hour to get ready before I can present myself at court. How many guests will there be at the feast, my little dove? And how many rooms shall I have in the palace? And what color are the lanterns, or does light shine from the gems themselves in the Kingdom of the Mountain Dragons?"

"Alas!" said Precious Jade, "my father is a prisoner and I am only an exile."

"Pshaw!" exclaimed the old woman, "what a daughter-in-law for you to bring back, you senseless oaf! Look at the robe she is wearing, and her hands are fit for nothing! Go and bring me a pail of water, you useless girl! As for you," she cried, turning to her son, "you shall feel if my old arms are withered yet!" And she caught up her broom and began belaboring him with it.

"*A thin horse has long hair*," remarked Wang Li philosophically when she had done, and he went out into the garden to find her a peach to refresh her after so much effort.

"I shall have to make the best of it," she grumbled to herself, when she had eaten the peach. "The boy has ears of stone. He follows his own way. If the mountain will not turn, I must be the road and do the turning myself." After that she was kind to Precious Jade, who tried to be of help to her mother-in-law in every possible way.

So they lived together in peace and happiness, working hard, incurring no debts, and showing kindness to all. Throughout the district the rains fell punctually, no one had any complaint of Roving Horse River, and the earth was no longer shaken by the burrowing of dragons. In time Precious Jade bore a beautiful son whom they named Little Splendor and there were never four happier people in the world. One day, not long afterwards, as Wang Li and Precious Jade sat alone beneath a grapevine trellis which Wang Li had recently made, Precious Jade began, laying down her embroidery:

"My dear husband, a message has reached me from my father. It seems that my unworthy uncle, issuing forth hastily from his palace, struck himself against the point of your spear and after some time died. My father is again on his jewel throne, and naturally feels a deep gratitude towards you." She paused.

"Now you are going to tell me about the palaces under the mountains which I may have for the asking," said Wang Li.

"I always hated palaces. There was never anything to do," said Precious Jade, smiling. Then she went back to her embroidery.

"My husband is the proudest man in the world," she remarked to a yellow silk butterfly which she had not quite finished.

"Proud?" asked Wang Li, "yet here I am and I might be a prince."

"You're too proud to be a prince," she replied, "and that is why I love you. I always wanted to marry the proudest man in the world."

"Maybe it's pride and maybe it's wisdom," said Wang Li, "but there are palaces and terraces of the mind I would not exchange for all the riches of the dragons."

And Precious Jade understood. In time Wang Li became so famous for his wisdom and benevolence that sages traveled from the farthest provinces to walk with him as he followed his plow. But sometimes when he was busy and the old mother needed a new silk gown or the baby wanted sweetmeats, Precious Jade would softly shake the leaves of the tree beside the door, and down would fall a light shower of silver coins. And Wang Li never noticed what it was that Precious Jade gathered under the mulberry tree.

St. George
and the Dragon

retold by William II. G. Kingston

THE HERMIT WELCOMED St. George and De Fistycuff. He was a venerable man, with a long beard of silvery whiteness; and as he tottered forward he seemed bowed almost to the ground with the weight of years.

"Gladly will I afford you shelter and such food as my cell can furnish, most gallant Knight," he said; and, suiting the action to the word, he placed a variety of provisions on the table. "I need not inquire to what country you belong, for I see by the arms of England engraven on your burgonet whence you come. I know the knights of that land are brave and gallant, and ready to do battle in aid of the distressed. Here, then, you will find an

opportunity for distinguishing yourself by a deed which will make your name renowned throughout the world."

St. George pricked up his ears at this, and eagerly inquired what it was. "This, you must understand, most noble Knight, is the renowned territory of Bagabornabou, second to none in the world in importance in the opinion of its inhabitants. None was so prosperous, none so flourishing, when a most horrible misfortune befell the land, in the appearance of a terrific green dragon, of huge proportions, who ranges up and down the country, creating devastation and dismay in every direction. No corner of the land is safe from his ravages; no one can hope to escape the consequences of his appearance. Every day his insatiable maw must be fed with the body of a young maiden, while so pestiferous is the breath which exhales from his throat that it causes a plague of a character so violent that whole districts have been depopulated by it. He commences his career of destruction at dawn every morning, and till his victim is ready he continues to ravage the land. When he has swallowed his lamentable repast he remains asleep till next morning, and then he proceeds as before.

"Many attempts have been made to capture him during the night, but he has invariably destroyed the brave men who have gone out to attack him, and has swallowed them for his supper. For no less than twenty-four long years has this dreadful infliction been suffered by our beloved country, till scarcely a maiden remains alive, nor does a brave man continue in it. The most lovely and perfect of her sex, the King's only daughter, the charming Sabra, is to be made an offering to the fell dragon tomorrow, unless a knight can be found gallant and brave enough to risk his life in mortal combat with the monster, and with skill and strength sufficient to destroy him.

"The King has promised, in his royal word, that, should such a knight appear and come off victorious, he will give him his daughter in marriage and the crown of Bagabornabou at his decease."

"Ah!" exclaimed the English Knight, his whole countenance beaming with satisfaction, "here is a deed to be done truly worthy of my prowess! I fully purpose to kill the dragon and rescue the Princess."

The daring Knight and his faithful Squire now entered the valley where the terrific green dragon had his abode. No sooner did the fiery eyes of the hideous monster fall on the steel-clad warrior instead of the fair maiden he expected to see, than from his leathern throat he sent forth a cry of rage louder and more tremendous than thunder, and arousing himself he prepared for the contest about to occur. As he reared up on his hind legs with his wings outspread, and his long scaly tail, with a huge red fork, extending far away behind him, his sharp claws wide open, each of the size of a large ship's anchor, his gaping mouth armed with double rows of huge teeth, between which appeared a fiery red tongue, and vast eyes blazing like burning coals, while his nostrils spouted forth fire, and the upper part of his body was covered with glittering green scales brighter than polished silver, and harder than brass, the under part being of a deep golden hue—his appearance might well have made even one of the bravest of men unwilling to attack him.

St. George trembled not, but thought of the lovely Sabra, and nerved himself for the encounter. De Fistycuff did not like his looks, and had he been alone would have been tempted to beat a retreat, but his love for his master kept him by his side.

"See," said the hermit, who had come thus far, "there is the dragon! He is a monster huge and horrible; but I believe that, like other monsters, by bravery and skill he can be overcome. See, the valley is full of fruit trees! Should he wound you, and should you be faint, you will find one bearing

oranges of qualities so beneficial, that, should you be able to procure one plucked fresh from the tree, it will instantly revive you. Now, farewell! See, the brute is approaching!"

On came the monster dragon, flapping his wings, spouting fire from his nostrils, and roaring loudly with his mouth. St. George couched his sharp spear and, spurring his steed, dashed onward to the combat. So terrific was the shock that the Knight was almost hurled from his saddle, while his horse, driven back on his haunches, lay, almost crushed, beneath the monster's superincumbent weight; but both man and steed extricating themselves with marvelous agility, St. George made another thrust of his spear, with all his might, against the scaly breast of the dragon. He might as well have struck against a gate of brass.

In a moment the stout spear was shivered into a thousand fragments, and the dragon uttered a loud roar of derision. At the same time, to show what he could do, he whisked round his venomous pointed tail with so rapid a movement that he brought both man and horse to the ground.

There they lay, almost senseless from the blow, while the dragon retreated backward some hundred paces or more, with the intention of coming back with greater force than before, and completing the victory he had almost won. Happily De Fistycuff divined the monster's purpose, and seeing one of the orange trees of which the hermit had spoken, he picked an orange and hurried with it to his master.

Scarcely had the Knight tasted it than he felt his strength revive, and leaping to his feet, he gave the remainder of it to his trusty steed, on whose back instantly mounting, he stood prepared, with his famous sword Ascalon in his hand, to receive the furious charge which the dragon was about to make.

Though his spear had failed him at a pinch, his trusty falchion was true as ever; and making his horse spring forward, he struck the monster such a blow on his golden-colored breast that the point entered between the scales, inflicting a wound which made it roar with pain and rage.

Slight, however, was the advantage which the Knight thereby gained, for there issued forth from the wound so copious a stream of black gore, with an odor so terrible, that it drove him back, almost drowning him and his brave steed, while the noxious fumes, entering their nostrils, brought them both fainting and helpless to the ground.

De Fistycuff, mindful of his master's commands, narrowly eyed the dragon, to see what he was about to do. Stanching his wound with a touch of his fiery tail, he flapped his green wings, roaring hoarsely, and shook his vast body, preparatory to another attack on the Knight.

"Is that it?" cried the Squire; and running to the orange tree, whence he plucked a couple of the golden fruit, he poured the juice of one down the throat of his master, and of the other down that of Bayard. Both revived in an instant, and St. George, springing on Bayard's back, felt as fresh and ready for the fight as ever. Both had learned the importance of avoiding the dragon's tail, and when he whisked it on one side Bayard sprang to the other, and so on, backwards and forwards, nimbly avoiding the blows aimed by the venomous instrument at him or his rider.

Again and again the dragon reared itself up, attempting to drop down and crush his gallant assailant; but Bayard, with wonderful sagacity, comprehending exactly what was to be done, sprung backwards or aside each time the monster descended, and thus avoided the threatened catastrophe. Still the dragon appeared as able as ever to endure the combat. St. George saw that a strenuous effort must be made, and taking a fresh grasp of Ascalon, he spurred onward to meet the monster, who once more advanced, with outstretched wings, with the full purpose of destroying him. This time St. George kept his spurs in the horse's flanks. "Death or victory must be the result of this change," he shouted to De Fistycuff.

With Ascalon's bright point kept well before him, he drove directly at the breast of the monster. The sword struck him under the wing; through the thick flesh it went, and nothing stopped it till it pierced the monster's heart. Uttering a loud groan, which resounded through the neighboring woods and mountains, and made even the wild beasts tremble with consternation, the furious green dragon fell over on its side, when St. George, drawing his falchion from the wound, dashed on over the prostrate form of the monster, and, ere it could rise to revenge itself on its destroyer, with many a blow he severed the head from the body. So vast was the stream which flowed forth from the wound that the whole valley speedily became a lake of blood, and the river which ran down from it first gave notice, by its sanguineous hue, to the inhabitants of the neighboring districts that the noble Champion of England had slain their long-tormenting enemy.

Stan Bolovan

retold by Andrew Lang

ONCE UPON A time what happened did happen, and if it had not happened this story would never have been told.

On the outskirts of a village just where the oxen were turned out to pasture, and the pigs roamed about burrowing with their noses among the roots of the trees, there stood a small house. In the house lived a man who had a wife, and the wife was sad all day long.

"Dear wife, what is wrong with you that you hang your head like a drooping rosebud?" asked her husband one morning. "You have everything you want; why cannot you be merry like other women?"

"Leave me alone, and do not seek to know the reason," replied she, bursting into tears, and the man thought that it was no time to question her, and went away to his work.

He could not, however, forget all about it, and a few days after he inquired again the reason of her sadness, but only got the same reply. At length he felt he could bear it no longer, and tried a third time, and then his wife turned and answered him.

"Good gracious!" cried she, "why cannot you let things be as they are? If I were to tell you, you would become just as wretched as myself. If you would only believe, it is far better for you to know nothing."

But no man yet was ever content with such an answer. The more you beg him not to inquire, the greater is his curiosity to learn the whole.

"Well, if you *must* know," said the wife at last, "I will tell you. There is no luck in this house—no luck at all!"

"Is not your cow the best milker in all the village? Are not your trees as full of fruit as your hives are full of bees? Has anyone cornfields like ours? Really you talk nonsense when you say things like that!"

"Yes, all that you say is true, but we have no children."

Then Stan understood, and when a man once understands and has his eyes opened it is no longer well with him. From that day the little house in the outskirts contained an unhappy man as well as an unhappy woman. And at the sight of her husband's misery the woman became more wretched than ever.

And so matters went on for some time.

Some weeks had passed, and Stan thought he would consult a wise man who lived a day's journey from his own house. The wise man was sitting before his door when he came up, and Stan fell on his knees before him. "Give me children, my lord, give me children."

"Take care what you are asking," replied the wise man. "Will not children be a burden to you? Are you rich enough to feed and clothe them?"

"Only give them to me, my lord, and I will manage somehow!" and at a sign from the wise man Stan went his way.

He reached home that evening tired and dusty, but with hope in his heart. As he drew near his house a sound of voices struck upon his ear, and he looked up to see the whole place full of children. Children in the garden, children in the yard, children looking out of every window—it seemed to the man as if all the children in the world must be gathered there. And none was bigger than the other, but each was smaller than the other, and every one was more noisy and more impudent and more daring than the rest, and Stan gazed and grew cold with horror as he realized that they all belonged to him.

"Good gracious! How many there are! How many!" he muttered to himself.

"Oh, but not one too many," smiled his wife, coming up with a crowd more children clinging to her skirts.

But even she found that it was not so easy to look after a hundred children, and when a few days had passed and they had eaten up all the food there was in the house, they began to cry, "Father! I am hungry—I am hungry," till Stan scratched his head and wondered what he was to do next. It was not that he thought there were too many children, for his life had seemed more full of joy since they appeared, but now it came to the point he did not know how he was to feed them. The cow had ceased to give milk, and it was too early for the fruit trees to ripen.

"Do you know, old woman!" said he one day to his wife, "I must go out into the world and try to bring back food somehow, though I cannot tell where it is to come from."

To the hungry man any road is long, and then there was always the thought that he had to satisfy a hundred greedy children as well as himself.

Stan wandered, and wandered, and wandered, till he reached to the end of the world, where that which is, is mingled with that which is not, and there he saw, a little way off, a sheepfold, with seven sheep in it. In the shadow of some trees lay the rest of the flock.

Stan crept up, hoping that he might manage to decoy some of them away quietly and drive them home for food for his family, but he soon found this could not be. For at midnight he heard a rushing noise, and through the air flew a dragon, who drove apart a ram, a sheep, and a lamb, and three fine cattle that were lying down close by. And besides these he took the milk of seventy-seven sheep, and carried it home to his old mother, that she might bathe in it and grow young again. And this happened every night.

The shepherd bewailed himself in vain: the dragon only laughed, and Stan saw that this was not the place to get food for his family.

But though he quite understood that it was almost hopeless to fight against such a powerful monster, yet the thought of the hungry children at home clung to him like a burr, and would not be shaken off, and at last he said to the shepherd, "What will you give me if I rid you of the dragon?"

"One of every three rams, one of every three sheep, one of every three lambs," answered the herd.

"It is a bargain," replied Stan, though at the moment he did not know how, supposing he *did* come off the victor, he would ever be able to drive so large a flock home.

However, that matter could be settled later. At present night was not far off, and he must consider how best to fight with the dragon.

Just at midnight, a horrible feeling that was new and strange to him came over Stan—a feeling that he could not put into words even to himself, but which almost forced him to give up the battle and take the shortest road home again. He half turned; then he remembered the children, and turned back.

"You or I," said Stan to himself, and took up his position on the edge of the flock.

"Stop!" he suddenly cried, as the air was filled with a rushing noise, and the dragon came dashing past.

"Dear me!" exclaimed the dragon, looking round. "Who are you, and where do you come from?"

"I am Stan Bolovan, who eats rocks all night, and in the day feeds on the flowers of the mountains; and if you meddle with those sheep I will carve a cross on your back."

When the dragon heard these words he stood quite still in the middle of the road, for he knew he had met with his match.

"But you will have to fight me first," he said in a trembling voice, for when you faced him properly he was not brave at all.

"I fight you?" replied Stan, "why I could slay you with one breath!" Then, stooping to pick up a large cheese which lay at his feet, he added, "Go and get a stone like this out of the river, so that we may lose no time in seeing who is the best man."

The dragon did as Stan bade him, and brought back a stone out of the brook.

"Can you get buttermilk out of your stone?" asked Stan.

The dragon picked up his stone with one hand, and squeezed it till it fell into powder, but no buttermilk flowed from it. "Of course I can't!" he said, half angrily.

"Well, if you can't, I can," answered Stan, and he pressed the cheese till buttermilk flowed through his fingers.

When the dragon saw that, he thought it was time he made the best of his way home again, but Stan stood in his path.

"We have still some accounts to settle," said he, "about what you have been doing here," and the poor dragon was too frightened to stir, lest Stan should slay him at one breath and bury him among the flowers in the mountain pastures.

"Listen to me," he said at last, "I see you are a very useful person, and my mother has need of a fellow like you. Suppose you enter her service for three days, which are as long as one of your years, and she will pay you each day seven sacks full of ducats."

Three times seven sacks full of ducats! The offer was very tempting, and Stan could not resist it. He did not waste words, but nodded to the dragon, and they started along the road.

It was a long, long way, but when they came to the end they found the dragon's mother, who was as old as time itself, expecting them. Stan saw her eyes shining like lamps from afar, and when they entered the house they beheld a huge kettle standing on the fire, filled with milk. When the old mother found that her son had arrived empty-handed she grew very angry, and fire and flame darted from her nostrils, but before she could speak the dragon turned to Stan.

"Stay here," said he, "and wait for me; I am going to explain things to my mother."

Stan was already repenting bitterly that he had ever come to such a place, but, since he was there, there was nothing for it but to take everything quietly, and not show that he was afraid.

"Listen, mother," said the dragon as soon as they were alone, "I have brought this man in order to get rid of him. He is a terrific fellow who eats rocks, and can press buttermilk out of a stone," and he told her all that had happened the night before.

"Oh, just leave him to me!" she said. "I have never yet let a man slip through my fingers." So Stan had to stay and do the old mother service.

The next day she told him that he and her son should try which was the strongest, and she took down a huge club, bound seven times with iron.

The dragon picked it up as if it had been a feather, and, after whirling it round his head, flung it lightly three miles away, telling Stan to beat that if he could.

They walked to the spot where the club lay. Stan stooped and felt it; then a great fear came over him, for he knew that he and all his children together would never lift that club from the ground.

"What are you doing?" asked the dragon.

"I was thinking what a beautiful club it was, and what a pity it is that it should cause your death."

"How do you mean—my death?" asked the dragon.

"Only that I am afraid that if I throw it you will never see another dawn. You don't know how strong I am!"

"Oh, never mind that—be quick and throw."

"If you are really in earnest, let us go and feast for three days: that will at any rate give you three extra days of life."

Stan spoke so calmly that this time the dragon began to get a little frightened, though he did not quite believe that things would be as bad as Stan said.

They returned to the house, took all the food that could be found in the old mother's larder, and carried it back to the place where the club was lying. Then Stan seated himself on the sack of provisions, and remained quietly watching the setting moon.

"What are you doing?" asked the dragon.

"Waiting till the moon gets out of my way."

"What do you mean? I don't understand."

"Don't you see that the moon is exactly in my way? But of course, if you like, I will throw the club into the moon."

At these words the dragon grew uncomfortable for the second time. He prized the club, which had been left him by his grandfather, very highly, and had no desire that it should be lost in the moon.

"I'll tell you what," he said, after thinking a little. "Don't throw the club at all. I will throw it a second time, and that will do just as well."

"No, certainly not!" replied Stan. "Just wait till the moon sets."

But the dragon, in dread lest Stan should fulfill his threats, tried what bribes could do, and in the end had to promise Stan seven sacks of ducats before he was suffered to throw back the club himself.

"Oh, dear me, that is indeed a strong man," said the dragon, turning to his mother. "Would you believe that I have had the greatest difficulty in preventing him from throwing the club into the moon?"

Then the old woman grew uncomfortable too! Only to think of it! It was no joke to throw things into the moon! So no more was heard of the club, and the next day they had all something else to think about.

"Go and fetch me water!" said the mother, when the morning broke, and gave them twelve buffalo skins with the order to keep filling them till night.

They set out at once for the brook, and in the twinkling of an eye the dragon had filled the whole twelve, carried them into the house, and brought them back to Stan. Stan was tired: he could scarcely lift the buckets when they were empty, and he shuddered to think of what would happen when they were full. But he only took an old knife out of his pocket and began to scratch up the earth near the brook.

"What are you doing there? How are you going to carry the water into the house?" asked the dragon.

"How? Dear me, that is easy enough! I shall just take the brook!"

At these words the dragon's jaw dropped. This was the last thing that had ever entered his head, for the brook had been as it was since the days of his grandfather.

"I'll tell you what!" he said. "Let me carry your skins for you."

"Most certainly not," answered Stan, going on with his digging, and the dragon, in dread lest he should fulfill his threat, tried what bribes would do, and in the end had again to promise seven sacks of ducats before Stan would agree to leave the brook alone and let him carry the water into the house.

On the third day the old mother sent Stan into the forest for wood, and, as usual, the dragon went with him.

Before you could count three he had pulled up more trees than Stan could have cut down in a lifetime, and had arranged them neatly in rows. When the dragon had finished, Stan began to look about him, and, choosing the biggest of the trees, he climbed up it, and breaking off a long rope of wild vine, bound the top of the tree to the one next it. And so he did to a whole line of trees.

"What are you doing there?" asked the dragon.

"You can see for yourself," answered Stan, going quietly on with his work.

"Why are you tying the trees together?"

"Not to give myself unnecessary work; when I pull up one, all the others will come up too."

"But how will you carry them home?"

"Dear me! Don't you understand that I am going to take the whole forest back with me?" said Stan, tying two other trees as he spoke.

"I'll tell you what," cried the dragon, trembling with fear at the thought

of such a thing; "let me carry the wood for you, and you shall have seven times seven sacks full of ducats."

"You are a good fellow, and I agree to your proposal," answered Stan, and the dragon carried the wood.

Now the three days' service which were to be reckoned as a year were over, and the only thing that disturbed Stan was how to get all those ducats back to his home!

In the evening the dragon and his mother had a long talk, but Stan heard every word through a crack in the ceiling.

"Woe be to us, mother," said the dragon; "this man will soon get us into his power. Give him his money, and let us be rid of him."

But the old mother was fond of money, and did not like this.

"Listen to me," said she; "you must murder him this very night."

"I am afraid," answered he.

"There is nothing to fear," replied the old mother. "When he is asleep take the club, and hit him on the head with it. It is easily done."

And so it would have been, had not Stan heard all about it. And when the dragon and his mother had put out their lights, he took the pigs' trough and filled it with earth, and placed it in his bed, and covered it with clothes. Then he hid himself underneath, and began to snore loudly.

Very soon the dragon stole softly into the room, and gave a tremendous blow on the spot where Stan's head should have been. Stan groaned loudly from under the bed, and the dragon went away as softly as he had come. Directly he had closed the door, Stan lifted out the pigs' trough, and lay down himself, after making everything clean and tidy, but he was wise enough not to shut his eyes that night.

The next morning he came into the room when the dragon and his mother were having their breakfast.

"Good morning," said he.

"Good morning. How did you sleep?"

"Oh, very well, but I dreamed that a flea had bitten me, and I seem to feel it still."

The dragon and his mother looked at each other. "Do you hear that?" whispered he. "He talks of a flea. I broke my club on his head."

This time the mother grew as frightened as her son. There was nothing to be done with a man like this, and she made all haste to fill the sacks with ducats, so as to get rid of Stan as soon as possible. But on his side Stan was trembling like an aspen, as he could not lift even one sack from the ground. So he stood still and looked at them.

"What are you standing there for?" asked the dragon.

"Oh, I was standing here because it has just occurred to me that I should like to stay in your service for another year. I am ashamed that when I get home they should see I have brought back so little. I know that they will cry out, 'Just look at Stan Bolovan, who in one year has grown as weak as a dragon.'"

Here a shriek of dismay was heard both from the dragon and his mother, who declared they would give him seven or even seven times seven the number of sacks if he would only go away.

"I'll tell you what!" said Stan at last. "I see you don't want me to stay, and I should be very sorry to make myself disagreeable. I will go at once, but only on condition that you shall carry the money home yourself, so that I may not be put to shame before my friends."

The words were hardly out of his mouth before the dragon had snatched up the sacks and piled them on his back. Then he and Stan set forth.

The way, though really not far, was yet too long for Stan, but at length he heard his children's voices, and stopped short. He did not wish the dragon to know where he lived, lest some day he should come to take back his

treasure. Was there nothing he could say to get rid of the monster? Suddenly an idea came into Stan's head, and he turned round.

"I hardly know what to do," said he. "I have a hundred children, and I am afraid they may do you harm, as they are always ready for a fight. However, I will do my best to protect you."

A hundred children! That was indeed no joke! The dragon let fall the sacks from terror, and then picked them up again. But the children, who had had nothing to eat since their father had left them, came rushing towards him, waving knives in their right hands and forks in their left, and crying, "Give us dragon's flesh; we will have dragon's flesh."

At this dreadful sight the dragon waited no longer: he flung down his sacks where he stood and took flight as fast as he could, so terrified at the fate that awaited him that from that day he has never dared to show his face in the world again.

The Good Sword

retold by Ruth Bryan Owen

FOR MANY YEARS a shepherd and his son lived on a lonely high-land, where they tended the sheep. Their low hut was scarcely higher than the thorny bushes around it. Beyond the grazing place there was a ring of mountains with dark rocks and deep caverns.

The old shepherd always avoided these mountains, and when the sheep wandered near them he made haste to turn them back.

Their life was a hard and lonely one but neither the shepherd nor his son wished to exchange it for any other. Father and son found contentment in each other's company and when the old man fell ill, the boy cared for him tenderly. After a time the old man felt his strength waning and one day he called his son to him and said, "I will soon have to leave you and I grieve that I can give you so small a heritage. Take down the old sword which hangs above our door."

The boy obeyed his father, although the sword felt very heavy in his hand. "This is all I have to give you," said his father. "Always keep it with you and remember that this sword will be victorious in any battle." And giving his son his blessing, the old man closed his eyes and did not open them again.

During the time of his great sorrow, while he was giving his father a proper burial, the son almost forgot about the rusty old sword which had been given to him; but when he closed the hut and drove the sheep down to the distant farm of the owner, the boy strapped the sword to his belt and soon got used to the feel of the heavy weight swinging at his side.

The farmer was surprised to see his flocks coming down from their pastures and bade the boy tell what had befallen his father, and when he had heard, the farmer said, "You are young to have charge of the flock by yourself, but I will let you try it for a while. One thing you must remember—do not let the sheep wander too near to the mountains. There are three pastures lying high on the mountainside which look so brightly green that your beasts may be tempted to clamber up to them, but three trolls live there and each has a small green meadow for himself. If your sheep should wander into one of the trolls' meadows, neither sheep nor shepherd would ever come back again."

The boy thought much of this warning as he drove the flock back toward their grazing place, and as they came nearer to the mountains he kept looking up toward the high green meadows. And in the days that followed, he looked many times toward the trolls' meadows.

Once, when he was tending his sheep, the boy thought suddenly of his sword. "Perhaps a fight with a troll would not be such a bad idea," he said to himself, and he did not drive the sheep back when they wandered toward the mountains. No sooner had the sheep strayed into the small green mead-ow than a fearful troll came roaring out of his cave. No one who has never seen a wicked troll can picture what an ugly and frightening sight it is.

"Do you know what happens to sheep and shepherds who trespass here?" the troll roared.

"If you mean to harm my sheep, I will have to give you a battle," said the boy, standing his ground.

When he saw how small the boy really was, the troll lashed himself about and breathed out great clouds of smoke. "Now is the time to use my sword," thought the shepherd boy, and as his enemy tried to lay hold of him he brought the sword down on the troll's head with such force that the creature was cut in half by the blow.

The sheep began pulling at the sweet grass of the first troll's meadow and were not content until they had cropped it short. Then they wandered toward the meadow of the second troll. The shepherd boy again did not hinder them and soon a troll far larger and more terrible than the first one came bellowing out of a cavern. "You have not only trespassed on my meadow, which makes your life forfeit, but you have also slain my brother and trampled down his grass."

"If you try to harm me or my sheep I will give you a battle," cried the boy, lifting up his sword.

The troll blew out such clouds of fire and smoke that the boy could scarcely see the frightful creature, but when he brought down his sword the troll was badly cut and died at once.

"Now my sheep have some fresh new grass," said the boy, but while his sheep were eating, he himself entered the third troll's meadow, sword in hand. The troll rushed out of his cavern with such howls of anger that the mountains trembled, but before the monster could say a word the boy rushed forward, crying, "It is your turn now!" and slew him with one blow.

When no troll was left living on the mountain, the boy could not wait to climb down into the great holes where they had lived. The three caverns met together under the earth, and when the shepherd boy came into this cave he saw a red horse with saddle and bridle set with rubies, a red dog which stood by the horse, and a suit of crimson armor that lay beside them. Nearby stood a yellow horse with topaz jewels on his harness. A yellow dog and a suit of yellow armor were beside this horse. In another corner of the cave a white horse and a white dog stood near a suit of white armor, and the horse's bridle and the white armor were studded thickly with pearls.

Great chests stood about the cave, filled with coins of silver and gold. It is no wonder that the boy, having slain the trolls and found all this treasure, was in high good spirits, and he went along singing as he drove the sheep back to their fold.

The farmer, who had come to the fold to find out how it was going with his young shepherd, not only found his sheep safe and bulging with food, but the shepherd boy himself, bubbling over with happiness.

"It is well that you and the flocks are prospering," said the farmer, "but I beg you to stop your singing when all our country is sharing in the King's sadness."

"Why should the King be sad?" asked the boy.

"It is all because of the three dreadful monsters," answered the farmer.

"Not the trolls who lived on our mountain, surely!" said the boy.

"No, it is the three dragons of the sea who are causing all this trouble, and they are larger and more terrible than the trolls on the mountain," said the farmer. "Even the King has no power against them and has finally had to promise that each of his three daughters shall be married to one of them. The King has promised a third of his property to anyone who will rid the kingdom of these dragons. It is said by all that the King is himself without any hope of rescue. It is not proper for you to be singing when everyone else is sorrowful," chided the farmer, as he turned back to his farm.

"The sheep will have to take care of themselves while I occupy myself with this matter," thought the shepherd, and when the farmer had gone the boy hastened to the cavern of the mountain trolls and put on the red armor and mounted himself on the red horse. Then calling to the red dog to follow him, he rode down to the seashore where the Princesses were to be given to the sea monsters.

In a little while the royal coach came along, and when it had stopped, a Princess stepped out, with a chamberlain beside her. As she stood there, pale with fear, a dragon rose up out of the sea. The chamberlain took one look at its three horrid heads and fled away and hid himself in some thick bushes.

Before the dragon could come near, the trembling Princess saw a horseman on a red horse draw his sword and cut off all three of the dragon's heads. He only stopped to cut the tongues from each of the heads, and rode away again with a red dog following after him.

When he saw that the danger was past, the chamberlain crawled from his hiding place and took charge of everything. "Climb back into the coach," he said to the Princess, "and be sure to let the King know that it was I who saved you. If you do not do this something more dreadful than a dragon will punish you," and the poor Princess, who was not yet over her fear, promised to say nothing at all about the red horseman.

A week later another Princess was to be delivered to the second sea dragon, and this time the shepherd boy put on the yellow armor and mounted the yellow horse, and with the yellow dog following behind him, he rode to the seashore and waited for the second Princess to arrive. Again a dragon came out onto the sands and it was hideous and terrible with six heads, and the chamberlain who had come with the second Princess ran away and hid himself at a safe distance.

The horseman rode forward and slashed the dragon to bits with his sword and then rode away, after he had cut out the dragon's six tongues.

After it was all over, the chamberlain took courage and came back to the Princess, threatening her with dreadful punishment if she should fail to tell the King that it was he himself who had slain the dragon.

"Say nothing about the yellow knight if you value your life," he said, and the second Princess had to do as the chamberlain directed.

When another week had passed, the shepherd boy dressed himself in the white armor and mounted the white horse, and with the white dog following him, he rode to the beach where the youngest Princess was to be given as a bride to the third sea dragon. This time, the dragon which rose up from the water had nine heads. It is not to be wondered at that the third chamberlain, who had ridden in the royal coach with the youngest Princess, fled away and scrambled up a tree at the first sight of the dreadful creature.

But the Princess, who had been looking all around in the hope that some rescuer would appear, spied the white horseman, and she watched him so intently that she scarcely noticed the dragon until after it had lost all of its nine heads and the white horseman was cutting out its nine tongues, one by one. And because she had not been frightened at the dragon she was only angry when the chamberlain came scurrying back down the tree trunk, and she was not at all ready to listen to him.

"Come here, brave knight," she called to the horseman, and before the chamberlain could notice, she slipped a little gold chain around her rescuer's neck. Then the horseman rode away and the third chamberlain came hurrying with threats of the harm that would come to her if she should fail to name him as her rescuer.

When the youngest Princess was returned safely to the palace there was great rejoicing, and the three dishonest chamberlains were praised for their courage and promised a rich reward.

"Each of you shall marry the Princess whom he rescued, and have a third of my kingdom," said the King, ordering a holiday and a festival for the Court, and all the people as well.

When the public holiday was proclaimed the shepherd boy asked the farmer if he, too, might take the day for himself.

"Certainly! The King's decree applies even to the humblest," the farmer said, as he gave him leave to join the merrymaking in the village.

Before setting out the shepherd boy called the three dogs from the trolls' cavern, and, followed by a red, a yellow, and a white dog, he came to the village inn. All manner of people were gathered about and there was much talk about the feast which was being given at the castle.

"Wouldn't it be fine to eat some of the good bread they are having there!" exclaimed the innkeeper.

"It would indeed," said the boy, "and it is possible that my dog could find some of the bread for us." So he said to the red dog, "Go to the castle and bring me some of the fine wheat bread they are eating there."

The dog went to the castle, scratched on the doors until they were opened for him, and searched about until he found the King's kitchen. Here he seized a loaf of bread in his mouth, and although everyone tried to stop him, the red dog escaped and carried the bread back to the inn and gave it to his master.

After they had eaten the bread, the innkeeper said, "How would it be if we could eat some of the good roast beef from the castle?"

"That is a fine idea," said the boy. "Perhaps my yellow dog will go to the castle and bring some of it for us."

So the yellow dog started out, and when he had reached the castle kitchen he seized a whole roast of beef in his mouth. The cooks tried to stop him, and the kitchen boys chased him with spoons and ladles, but the yellow dog ran back to the inn and gave the beef to his master.

The next day, when the weddings were to take place, the innkeeper said, "How wonderful it would be to have a sip of wine from the King's table!"

"That would be a good idea," said the boy. "Surely my white dog could fetch a bottle of wine for us."

When he commanded, the white dog went to the castle and into the hall where all the wedding guests were seated at the King's table, and, before any one of the amazed guests could say a word, it snatched a bottle of wine and ran with it to the inn. When the youngest Princess saw the white dog she clapped her hands and cried, "It was that white dog's master who saved me from the dragon!"

"What nonsense is this?" her bridegroom cried, angrily. "You know quite well that it was I who saved you."

"You have tried to make it appear so," said the Princess, "but now that I see the white dog, I know his master must be near. If you persist in your wicked stories he will serve you as he served the dragon. I will follow the white dog until I find my rescuer," and the Princess jumped up from the table.

"Let us all follow the dog," cried the King, and he and all the lords and ladies of the Court rushed out, too, and followed the dog to the inn. The shepherd boy was much astonished to see all the crowd and wanted to hide himself, but the youngest Princess cried, "My golden chain will be found around the neck of the man who killed the dragon," and the shepherd boy showed the golden chain which he had under his shirt.

But the third chamberlain began to shout, "Ho! Ho! How can this boy pretend that he has slain the dragon when I have the proof that I did it," and he brought in the nine heads of the last dragon which had been killed.

"My rescuer took the tongues from the dragon's heads," said the Princess, and the shepherd boy showed them not only the nine tongues which he had cut from this dragon's heads, but also the tongues from the heads of the other two dragons, so that no one could be in doubt about the matter any longer.

The three chamberlains were led away in disgrace to receive punishment for their crimes, and the shepherd boy set off for the castle, hand in hand with the youngest Princess, to whom he was married amid great rejoicing.

But he did not forget how much he owed to the good sword, and he had it hung up in a place of honor, for even a King feels a little more secure when he has a sword which can be trusted to win every battle for him.

The Dragon of Wantley

anonymous

Old stories tell, how Hercules,
A dragon slew at Lerna,
With seven heads, and fourteen eyes,
To see and well discern-a:
But he had a club, this dragon to drub,
Or he had ne'er done it, I warrant ye:
But More of More Hall, with nothing at all,
He slew the dragon of Wantley.

This dragon had two furious wings,
One upon each shoulder;
With a sting in his tail, as long as a flail,
Which made him bolder and bolder.
He had long claws, and in his jaws
Four-and-forty teeth of iron;
With a hide as tough as any buff,
And as strong as the jaws of a lion.

Have you not heard how the Trojan horse
Held seventy men in his belly?
This dragon was not quite so big,
But very near, I'll tell ye.
Devoured he poor children three,
That could not with him grapple;
And at one sup he ate them up,
As one would eat an apple.

All sorts of cattle this dragon did eat:
Some say he ate up trees,
And that the forests sure he would
Devour up by degrees:
Houses and churches like geese and turkeys
He ate all and left nothing behind
But some stones, dear Jack, that he could not crack,
Which on the hills you will find.

Hard by a furious knight there dwelt,
Men, women, girls, and boys,

Sighing and sobbing, came to his lodging,
And made a hideous noise:
"O save us all, More of More Hall,
Thou peerless knight of these woods;
Do but slay this dragon, who won't leave us a rag on,
We'll give thee all our goods."

This being done, he did engage
To hew the dragon down;
But first he went new armor to
Bespeak at Sheffield town;
With spikes all about, not within but without,
Of steel so sharp and strong;
Both behind and before, arms, legs, and all o'er,
 Some five or six inches long.

Had you but seen him in this dress,
How fierce he looked and how big,
You would have thought him for to be
Some Egyptian porcupig:
He frightened all, cats, dogs, and all,
Each cow, each horse, and each hog:
For fear they did flee, for they took him to be
Some strange, outlandish hedgehog.

To see this fight all people then
Got up on trees and houses,
On churches some, and chimneys too;
But these put on their trousers,

Not to spoil their hose. As soon as he rose,
To make him strong and mighty,
He drank, by the tale, six pots of ale
And a quart of aqua vitae.

It is not strength that always wins,
For wit doth strength excel;
Which made our cunning champion
Creep down into a well;
Where he did think, this dragon would drink,
And so he did in truth;
And as he stooped low, he rose up and cried "Boo!"
And hit him in the mouth.

"Oh," quoth the dragon, "come out, my man,
Thou disturb'st me in my drink."
And then he turned and breathed fire at him:
But the brave knight did not shrink.
"Beshrew thy soul, thy body's foul,
Thy breath smells not like balsam;
Thou evil beast with stifling breath,
Sure thy diet is unwholesome."

Our politic knight, on the other side,
Crept out upon the brink,
And gave the dragon such a douse,
He knew not what to think:
"By Jove," quoth he, "say you so, do you see?"
And then at him he let fly,

With hand and with foot, and so they went to't;
And the word it was, Hey, boys, hey!

"Your words," quoth the dragon, "I don't understand."
Then to it they fell at all,
Like two wild boars so fierce, if I may
Compare great things with small.
Two days and a night, with this dragon did fight
Our champion on the ground;
Tho' their strength it was great, their skill it was neat,
They never had one wound.

At length the hard earth began to quake,
The dragon gave him a knock,
Which made him to reel, and straightway he thought,
To lift him as high as a rock,
And thence let him fall. But More of More Hall,
Life a valiant knight in his pride,
As he came like a lout, so he turned him about,
And gave him a blow in the side.

"Oh," quoth the dragon, with a deep sigh,
And turned six times together,
Sobbing and tearing, cursing and swearing
Out of his throat of leather;
"More of More Hall! O thou rascal!
Would I had seen thee never;
With the thing at thy foot, thou hast slain me at the root,
And I'm quite undone forever."

"Murder, murder," the dragon cried,
"Alack, alack for grief;
Had you but missed that place, you could
Have done me no mischief."
Then his head he shaked, trembled, and quaked,
And down he laid and cried;
First on one knee, then on back tumbled he,
So groaned, kicked, shuddered, and died.

The Dragon Tamers

by E. Nesbit

THERE WAS ONCE an old, old castle. It was so old that its walls and towers and turrets and gateways and arches had crumbled to ruins, and of all its old splendor there were only two little rooms left, and it was here that John the blacksmith had set up his forge.

He was too poor to live in a proper house, and no one asked any rent for the rooms in the ruin, because all the lords of the castle were dead and gone this many a year. So there John blew his bellows, and hammered his iron, and did all the work which came his way.

This was not much, because most of the trade went to the mayor of the town, who was also a blacksmith in quite a large way of business, and had his huge forge facing the square of the town, and had twelve apprentices, all hammering like a nest of woodpeckers, and twelve journeymen to order the apprentices about, and a patent forge and a self-acting hammer and electric bellows, and all things handsome about him. So that of course the townspeople, whenever they wanted a horse shod or a shaft mended, went to the mayor. And John the blacksmith struggled on as best he could, with a few odd jobs from travelers and strangers who did not know what a superior forge the mayor's was.

The two rooms were warm and weathertight, but not very large, so the blacksmith got into the way of keeping his old iron, and his odds and ends, and his fagots, and his twopenn' worth of coal, in the great dungeon down under the castle. It was a very fine dungeon indeed, with a handsome vaulted roof and big iron rings, whose staples were built into the wall, very strong and convenient for tying captives up to, and at one end was a broken flight of wide steps leading down no one knew where.

Even the lords of the castle in the good old times had never known where those steps led to, but every now and then they would kick a prisoner down the steps in their lighthearted, hopeful way, and sure enough, the prisoners never came back. The blacksmith had never dared to go beyond the seventh step, and no more have I—so I know no more than he did what was at the bottom of those stairs.

John the blacksmith had a wife and a little baby. When his wife was not doing the housework she used to nurse the baby and cry, remembering the happy days when she lived with her father, who kept seventeen cows and lived quite in the country, and when John used to come courting her in the summer evenings, as smart as smart, with a posy in his buttonhole. And now John's hair was getting gray, and there was hardly ever enough to eat.

As for the baby, it cried a good deal at odd times, but at night, when its mother had settled down to sleep, it would always begin to cry, quite as a matter of course, so that she hardly got any rest at all. This made her very tired. The baby could make up for its bad nights during the day, if it liked, but the poor mother couldn't. So whenever she had nothing to do she used to sit and cry, because she was tired out with work and worry.

One evening the blacksmith was busy with his forge. He was making a goatshoe for the goat of a very rich lady, who wished to see how the goat liked being shod, and also whether the shoe would come to fivepence or sevenpence before she ordered the whole set. This was the only order John had had that week. And as he worked, his wife sat and nursed the baby, who, for a wonder, was not crying.

Presently, over the noise of the bellows, and over the clank of the iron, there came another sound. The blacksmith and his wife looked at each other.

"I heard nothing," said he.

"Neither did I," said she.

But the noise grew louder—and the two were so anxious not to hear it that he hammered away at the goatshoe harder than he had ever hammered in his life, and she began to sing to the baby—a thing she had not had the heart to do for weeks.

But through the blowing and hammering and singing the noise came louder and louder, and the more they tried not to hear it, the more they had to. It was like the noise of some great creature purring, purring, purring— and the reason they did not want to believe they really heard it was that it came from the great dungeon down below, where the old iron was, and the firewood and the twopenn' worth of coal, and the broken steps that went down into the dark and ended no one knew where.

"It *can't* be anything in the dungeon," said the blacksmith, wiping his face. "Why, I shall have to go down there after more coals in a minute."

"There isn't anything there, of course. How could there be?"said his wife. And they tried so hard to believe that there could be nothing there that presently they very nearly did believe it.

Then the blacksmith took his shovel in one hand and his riveting hammer in the other, and hung the old stable lantern on his little finger, and went down to get the coals.

"I am not taking the hammer because I think there is anything there," said he, "but it is handy for breaking the large lumps of coal."

"I quite understand," said his wife, who had brought the coal home in her apron that afternoon, and knew that it was all coal dust.

So he went down the winding stairs to the dungeon, and stood at the bottom of the steps holding the lantern above his head just to see that the dungeon really *was* empty, as usual. Half of it was empty as usual, except for the old iron and odds and ends, and the firewood and the coals. But the other side was not empty. It was quite full, and what it was full of was *Dragon*.

"It must have come up those nasty broken steps from goodness knows where," said the blacksmith to himself, trembling all over, as he tried to creep back up the winding stairs.

But the dragon was too quick for him—it put out a great claw and caught him by the leg, and as it moved it rattled like a great bunch of keys, or like the sheet iron they make thunder out of in pantomimes.

"No you don't," said the dragon, in a sputtering voice, like a damp squib.

"Deary, deary me," said poor John, trembling more than ever in the claw of the dragon. "Here's a nice end for a respectable blacksmith!"

The dragon seemed very much struck by this remark.

"Do you mind saying that again?" said he, quite politely.

So John said again, very distinctly, "Here—Is—A—Nice—End—For—A—Respectable—Blacksmith."

"I didn't know," said the dragon. "Fancy now! You're the very man I wanted."

"So I understood you to say before," said John, his teeth chattering.

"Oh, I don't mean what you mean," said the dragon, "but I should like you to do a job for me. One of my wings has got some of the rivets out of it just above the joint. Could you put that to rights?"

"I might, sir," said John, politely, for you must always be polite to a possible customer, even if he be a dragon.

"A master craftsman—you *are* a master, of course?—can see in a minute what's wrong," the dragon went on. "Just come round here and feel of my plates, will you?"

John timidly went round when the dragon took his claw away, and sure enough, the dragon's off wing was hanging loose and all anyhow, and several of the plates near the joint certainly wanted riveting.

The dragon seemed to be made almost entirely of iron armor—a sort of tawny, red-rust color it was; from damp, no doubt—and under it he seemed to be covered with something furry.

All the blacksmith welled up in John's heart, and he felt more at ease. "You could certainly do with a rivet or two, sir," said he. "In fact, you want a good many."

"Well, get to work, then," said the dragon. "You mend my wing, and then I'll go out and eat up all the town, and if you make a really smart job of it I'll eat you last. There!"

"I don't want to be eaten last, sir," said John.

"Well, then, I'll eat you *first*," said the dragon.

"I don't want that, sir, either," said John.

"Go on with you, you silly man," said the dragon. "You don't know your own silly mind. Come, set to work."

"I don't like the job, sir," said John, "and that's the truth. I know how easily accidents happen. It's all fair and smooth, and 'Please rivet me, and I'll eat you last'—and then you get to work and you give a gentleman a bit of a nip or a dig under his rivets—and then it's fire and smoke, and no apologies will meet the case."

"Upon my word of honor as a dragon," said the other.

"I know you wouldn't do it on purpose, sir," said John, "but any gentleman will give a jump and a sniff if he's nipped, and one of your sniffs would be enough for me. Now, if you'd just let me fasten you up?"

"It would be so undignified," objected the dragon.

"We always fasten a horse up," said John, "and he's the 'noble animal.'"

"It's all very well," said the dragon, "but how do I know you'd untie me again when you'd riveted me? Give me something in pledge. What do you value most?"

"My hammer," said John. "A blacksmith is nothing without a hammer."

"But you'd want that for riveting me. You must think of something else, and at once, or I'll eat you first."

At this moment the baby in the room above began to scream. Its mother had been so quiet that it thought she had settled down for the night, and that it was time to begin.

"Whatever's that?" said the dragon—starting so that every plate on his body rattled.

"It's only the baby," said John.

"What's that?" asked the dragon. "Something you value?"

"Well, yes, sir, rather," said the blacksmith.

"Then bring it here," said the dragon, "and I'll take care of it till you've done riveting me, and you shall tie me up."

"All right, sir," said John, "but I ought to warn you. Babies are poison to dragons, so I don't deceive you. It's all right to touch—but don't you go putting it into your mouth. I shouldn't like to see any harm come to a nice-looking gentleman like you."

The dragon purred at this compliment and said, "All right, I'll be careful. Now go and fetch the thing, whatever it is."

So John ran up the steps as quickly as he could, for he knew that if the dragon got impatient before it was fastened up, it could heave up the roof of the dungeon with one heave of its back, and kill them all in the ruins. His wife was asleep, in spite of the baby's cries, and John picked up the baby and took it down and put it between the dragon's front paws.

"You just purr to it, sir," he said, "and it'll be as good as gold."

So the dragon purred, and his purring pleased the baby so much that it left off crying.

Then John rummaged among the heap of old iron and found there some heavy chains and a great collar that had been made in the days when men sang over their work and put their hearts into it, so that the things they made were strong enough to bear the weight of a thousand years, let alone a dragon.

John fastened the dragon up with the collar and the chains, and when he had padlocked them all on safely, he set to work to find out how many rivets would be needed.

"Six, eight, ten—twenty, forty," said he. "I haven't half enough rivets in the shop. If you'll excuse me, sir, I'll step round to another forge and get a few dozen. I won't be a minute."

And off he went, leaving the baby between the dragon's forepaws, laughing and crowing with pleasure at the very large purr of it.

John ran as hard as he could into the town, and found the mayor and corporation.

"There's a dragon in my dungeon," he said. "I've chained him up. Now come and help to get my baby away."

And he told them all about it.

But they all happened to have engagements for that evening, so they praised John's cleverness, and said they were quite content to leave the matter in his hands.

"But what about my baby?" said John.

"Oh, well," said the mayor, "if anything should happen, you will always be able to remember that your baby perished in a good cause."

So John went home again and told his wife some of the tale.

"You've given the baby to the dragon!" she cried. "Oh, you unnatural parent!"

"Hush," said John, and he told her some more.

"Now," he said, "I'm going down. After I've been down you can go, and if you keep your head the boy will be all right."

So down went the blacksmith, and there was the dragon purring away with all his might to keep the baby quiet.

"Hurry up, can't you?" he said. "I can't keep up this noise all night."

"I'm very sorry, sir," said the blacksmith, "but all the shops are shut. The job must wait till the morning. And don't forget you've promised to take care of that baby. You'll find it a little wearing, I'm afraid. Good night, sir."

The dragon had purred till he was quite out of breath—so now he stopped, and as soon as everything was quiet the baby thought everyone must have settled for the night, and that it was time to begin to scream. So it began.

"Oh, dear," said the dragon, "this is awful."

He patted the baby with his claw, but it screamed more than ever.

"And I am so tired, too," said the dragon. "I did so hope I should have had a good night."

The baby went on screaming.

"There'll be no peace for me after this," said the dragon. "It's enough to ruin one's nerves. Hush, then—did 'ums, then." And he tried to quiet the baby as if it had been a young dragon. But when he began to sing "Hush-a-by, dragon," the baby screamed more and more and more. "I can't keep it quiet," said the dragon. And then suddenly he saw a woman sitting on the steps. "Here, I say," said he, "do you know anything about babies?"

"I do, a little," said the mother.

"Then I wish you'd take this one, and let me get some sleep," said the dragon, yawning. "You can bring it back in the morning before the blacksmith comes."

So the mother picked up the baby and took it upstairs and told her husband, and they went to bed happy, for they had caught the dragon and saved the baby.

And next day John went down and explained carefully to the dragon exactly how matters stood, and he got an iron gate with a grating to it, and set it up at the foot of the steps, and the dragon mewed furiously for days and days, but when he found it was no good he was quiet.

So now John went to the mayor, and said, "I've got the dragon and I've saved the town."

"Noble preserver," cried the mayor, "we will get up a subscription for you, and crown you in public with a laurel wreath."

So the mayor put his name down for five pounds, and the corporation each gave three, and other people gave their guineas and half guineas, and half crowns and crowns, and while the subscription was being made the mayor ordered three poems at his own expense from the town poet to celebrate the occasion. The poems were very much admired, especially by the mayor and corporation.

The first poem dealt with the noble conduct of the mayor in arranging to have the dragon tied up. The second described the splendid assistance rendered by the corporation. And the third expressed the pride and joy of the poet in being permitted to sing such deeds, beside which the actions of St. George must appear quite commonplace to all with feeling heart or a well-balanced brain.

When the subscription was finished there was a thousand pounds, and a committee was formed to settle what should be done with it. A third of it went to pay for a banquet to the mayor and corporation; another third was spent in buying a gold collar with a dragon on it for the mayor, and gold medals with dragons on them for the corporation; and what was left went in committee expenses.

So there was nothing left for the blacksmith except the laurel wreath, and the knowledge that it really *was* he who had saved the town. But after this things went a little better with the blacksmith. To begin with, the baby did not cry so much as it had before. Then the rich lady who owned the goat was so touched by John's noble action that she ordered a complete set of shoes at two shillings, fourpence, and even made it up to two shillings, sixpence, in grateful recognition of his public-spirited conduct. Then tourists used to come in breaks from quite a long way off, and pay twopence each to go down the steps and peep through the iron grating at the rusty dragon in the dungeon—and it was threepence extra for each party if the blacksmith let off colored fire to see it by, which, as the fire was extremely short, was twopence-halfpenny clear profit every time. And the blacksmith's wife used to provide teas at ninepence a head, and altogether things grew brighter week by week.

The baby—named John, after his father, and called Johnnie for short—began presently to grow up. He was great friends with Tina, the daughter of the whitesmith, who lived nearly opposite. She was a dear little girl, with yellow pigtails and blue eyes, and she was never tired of hearing the story of how Johnnie, when he was a baby, had been minded by a real dragon.

The two children used to go together to peep through the iron grating at the dragon, and sometimes they would hear him mew piteously. And they would light a halfpenny worth of colored fire to look at him by. And they grew older and wiser.

Now, at last one day the mayor and corporation, hunting hare in their gold gowns, came screaming back to the town gates with news that a lame, humpy giant, as big as a tin church, was coming over the marshes towards the town.

"We're lost," said the mayor. "I'd give a thousand pounds to anyone who could keep that giant out of the town. *I* know what he eats—by his teeth."

No one seemed to know what to do. But Johnnie and Tina were listening, and they looked at each other, and then ran off as fast as their boots would carry them.

They ran through the forge, and down the dungeon steps, and knocked at the iron door.

"Who's there?" said the dragon.

"It's only us," said the children.

And the dragon was so dull from having been alone for ten years that he said, "Come in, dears."

"You won't hurt us, or breathe fire at us or anything?" asked Tina.

And the dragon said, "Not for worlds."

So they went in and talked to him, and told him what the weather was like outside, and what there was in the papers, and at last Johnnie said, "There's a lame giant in the town. He wants you."

"Does he?" said the dragon, showing his teeth. "If only I were out of this!"

"If we let you loose you might manage to run away before he could catch you."

"Yes, I *might*," answered the dragon, "but then again I mightn't."

"Why—you'd never fight him?" said Tina.

"No," said the dragon. "I'm all for peace, I am. You let me out, and you'll see."

So the children loosed the dragon from the chains and the collar, and he broke down one end of the dungeon and went out—only pausing at the forge door to get the blacksmith to rivet his wing.

He met the lame giant at the gate of the town, and the giant banged on the dragon with his club as if he were banging an iron foundry, and the dragon behaved like a smelting works—all fire and smoke. It was a fearful sight, and people watched it from a distance, falling off their legs with the shock of every bang, but always getting up to look again.

At last the dragon won, and the giant sneaked away across the marshes, and the dragon, who was very tired, went home to sleep, announcing his intention of eating the town in the morning. He went back into his old dungeon because he was a stranger in the town, and he did not know of any other respectable lodging. Then Tina and Johnnie went to the mayor and corporation and said, "The giant is settled. Please give us the thousand pounds reward."

But the mayor said, "No, no, my boy. It is not you who have settled the giant, it is the dragon. I supposed you have chained him up again? When *he* comes to claim the reward he shall have it."

"He isn't chained up yet," said Johnnie. "Shall I send him to claim the reward?"

But the mayor said he need not trouble, and now he offered a thousand pounds to anyone who would get the dragon chained up again.

"I don't trust you," said Johnnie. "Look how you treated my father when he chained up the dragon."

But the people who were listening at the door interrupted, and said that if Johnnie could fasten up the dragon again they would turn out the mayor and let Johnnie be mayor in his place. For they had been dissatisfied with the mayor for some time, and thought they would like a change.

So Johnnie said, "Done," and off he went, hand in hand with Tina, and they called on all their little friends and said, "Will you help us save the town?"

And all the children said, "Yes, of course we will. What fun!"

"Well, then," said Tina, "you must all bring your basins of bread and milk to the forge tomorrow at breakfast time."

"And if ever I am mayor," said Johnnie, "I will give a banquet, and you shall all be invited. And we'll have nothing but sweet things from beginning to end."

All the children promised, and next morning Tina and Johnnie rolled the big washing tub down the winding stair.

"What's that noise?" asked the dragon.

"It's only a big giant breathing," said Tina. "He's gone by, now."

Then, when all the town children brought their bread and milk, Tina emptied it into the washtub, and when the tub was full Tina knocked at the iron door with the grating in it, and said, "May we come in?"

"Oh, yes," said the dragon; "it's very dull here."

So they went in, and with the help of nine other children they lifted the washing tub in and set it down by the dragon. Then all the other children went away, and Tina and Johnnie sat down and cried.

"What's this?" asked the dragon. "And what's the matter?"

"*This* is bread and milk," said Johnnie. "It's our breakfast—all of it."

"Well," said the dragon, "I don't see what you want with breakfast. I'm going to eat everyone in the town as soon as I've rested a little."

"Dear Mr. Dragon," said Tina, "I wish you wouldn't eat us. How would you like to be eaten yourself?"

"Not at all," the dragon confessed, "but nobody will eat me."

"I don't know," said Johnnie, "there's a giant—"

"I know. I fought with him, and licked him—"

"Yes, but there's another come now—the one you fought was only this one's little boy. This one is half as big again."

"He's seven times as big," said Tina.

"No, nine times," said Johnnie. "He's bigger than the steeple."

"Oh dear," said the dragon. "I never expected this."

"And the mayor has told him where you are," Tina went on, "and he is coming to eat you as soon as he has sharpened his big knife. The mayor told him you were a wild dragon—but he didn't mind. He said he only ate wild dragons—with bread sauce."

"That's tiresome," said the dragon, "and I suppose this sloppy stuff in the tub is the bread sauce?"

The children said it was. "Of course," they added, "bread sauce is only served with wild dragons. Tame ones are served with applesauce and onion stuffing. What a pity you're not a tame one: he'd never look at you then," they said. "Good-bye, poor dragon, we shall never see you again, and now you'll know what it's like to be eaten." And they began to cry again.

"Well, but look here," said the dragon, "couldn't you pretend I was a tame dragon? Tell the giant that I'm just a poor little, timid tame dragon that you keep for a pet."

"He'd never believe it," said Johnnie. "If you were our tame dragon we

should keep you tied up, you know. We shouldn't like to risk losing such a dear, pretty pet."

Then the dragon begged them to fasten him up at once, and they did so: with a collar and chains that were made years ago—in the days when men sang over their work and made it strong enough to bear any strain.

And then they went away and told the people what they had done, and Johnnie was made mayor, and had a glorious feast exactly as he had said he would—with nothing in it but sweet things. It began with Turkish delight and halfpenny buns, and went on with oranges, toffee, coconut ice, peppermints, jam puffs, raspberry noyau, ice creams, and meringues, and ended with bull's-eyes and gingerbread and acid drops.

This was all very well for Johnnie and Tina, but if you are kind children with feeling hearts you will perhaps feel sorry for the poor deceived, deluded dragon—chained up in the dull dungeon, with nothing to do but think over the shocking untruths that Johnnie had told him.

When he thought how he had been tricked, the poor captive dragon began to weep—and the large tears fell down over his rusty plates. And presently he began to feel faint, as people sometimes do when they have been crying, especially if they have not had anything to eat for ten years or so.

And then the poor creature dried his eyes and looked about him, and there he saw the tub of bread and milk. So he thought, "If giants like this damp, white stuff, perhaps *I* should like it too," and he tasted a little, and liked it so much that he ate it all up.

And the next time the tourists came, and Johnnie let off the colored fire, the dragon said, shyly, "Excuse my troubling you, but could you bring me a little more bread and milk?"

So Johnnie arranged that people should go round with carts every day to collect the children's bread and milk for the dragon. The children were fed at the town's expense—on whatever they liked. And they ate nothing but cakes and buns and sweet things, and they said the poor dragon was very welcome to their bread and milk.

Now, when Johnnie had been mayor ten years or so he married Tina, and on their wedding morning they went to see the dragon. He had grown quite tame, and his rusty plates had fallen off in places, and underneath he was soft and furry to stroke. So now they stroked him.

And he said, "I don't know how I could ever have liked eating anything but bread and milk. I *am* a tame dragon, now, aren't I?" And when they said yes, he was, the dragon said, "I am so tame, won't you undo me?"

And some people would have been afraid to trust him, but Johnnie and Tina were so happy on their wedding day that they could not believe any harm of anyone in the world. So they loosed the chains, and the dragon said, "Excuse me a moment, there are one or two little things I should like to fetch," and he moved off to those mysterious steps and went down them, out of sight into the darkness. And as he moved, more and more of his rusty plates fell off.

In a few minutes they heard him clanking up the steps. He brought something in his mouth—it was a bag of gold.

"It's no good to me," he said. "Perhaps you might find it come in useful." So they thanked him very kindly.

"More where that came from," said he, and fetched more and more and more, till they told him to stop. So now they were rich, and so were their fathers and mothers. Indeed, everyone was rich, and there were no more poor people in the town. And they all got rich without working, which is very wrong, but the dragon had never been to school, as you have, so he knew no better.

And as the dragon came out of the dungeon, following Johnnie and Tina into the bright gold and blue of their wedding day, he blinked his eyes as a cat does in the sunshine, and he shook himself, and the last of his plates dropped off, and his wings with them, and he was just like a very, very extra-sized cat. And from that day he grew furrier and furrier, and he was the beginning of all cats. Nothing of the dragon remained except the claws, which all cats have still, as you can easily ascertain.

And I hope you see now how important it is to feed your cat with bread and milk. If you were to let it have nothing to eat but mice and birds it might grow larger and fiercer, and scalier and tailier, and get wings and turn into the beginning of dragons. And then there would be all the bother over again.